BRIE'S SUBMISSION

Tied to Hope

Welcome home !

Red Phoenix

Red Phoenix

Tied to Hope: Brie's Submission
18th Book of the Brie Series

Cover by Shanoff Designs
Formatted by BB Books
Phoenix symbol by Nicole Delfs

Dedication

Oh, my friends, we have waited a long time to hear from Brie and I promise you this story is everything you are hoping for and more!

I have to thank my muses who continue to surprise, rip my heart out, and delight me.

Big thanks to my editor and friend, Kh Koehler. She knows the personal struggles I went through while writing this book and worked with me through them.

More shout outs to my amazing beta team who worked on a tight deadline to make this release the best it can be – Becki, Kathy, Marilyn and Brenda – love ya!

To my marketing team, Jon and Jessica, I can't tell you how wonderful it is to talk to you weekly (sometimes daily). Your creative ideas, hard work, and passion for my stories inspires me more than you know.

A huge shout out to MrRed who is the love of my life and supports my crazy hours in every way he can. This book wouldn't be out in the world if it hadn't been for his constant love, inspiration, and supportive efforts.

To my fans, how lucky I am to have you in my life! I never would have believed I'd be writing the 18th book in the Brie's Submission series and you would be as excited about it as you were the about the first book. You help bring every single person in the Brie series to life with your enthusiasm and dedication.

My heart is full. Thank you!

SIGN UP FOR MY NEWSLETTER HERE FOR THE LATEST RED PHOENIX UPDATES

SALES, GIVEAWAYS, NEW RELEASES, PREORDER LINKS, AND MORE!

SIGN UP HERE

REDPHOENIXAUTHOR.COM/NEWSLETTER-SIGNUP

Don't miss the Audiobook narrated by Pippa Jayne!

Tied to Hope:
Brie's Submission #18
Available Soon

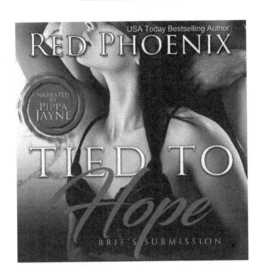

CONTENTS

Welcome Home

As Brie stepped up to the porch, holding Hope in her arms, the door to their new home swung open. To her shock and delight, Rytsar stood in front of her with Titov behind him.

Wearing a mischievous grin, the Russian threw his arms wide open and commanded, "*Radost moya,* welcome me home."

Brie stood frozen in shock for a moment, then rushed into his arms. "Rytsar!"

The tears started when she melted into his powerful embrace.

"No tears," he chuckled as he looked down at her and the baby. "This is a happy occasion, is it not?"

She nodded, smiling, as she hastily wiped away her tears with her free hand. "I...I just can't believe you're here. You've been gone so long…"

"I had to finish it," he answered, grazing the baby's cheek with his thumb. "For you and for *moye solntse.*"

Brie looked at him in happy disbelief, barely choking

out the words, "You're home..." before the tears starting falling again.

He gave Sir, who was standing beside her, a cha-grinned look. "Your submissive is still not very good at following commands."

"In this instance, I'll give her leniency," Sir stated with a grin, sticking out his hand to Rytsar. "Welcome home, brother."

Rytsar grasped it, pulling him close. He wrapped his arm around Sir with his other arm still around Brie.

Volumes were spoken between the two men without either saying a word.

Brie had given Rytsar up for lost after the long peri-od of silence, and she couldn't quite believe he was here in the flesh.

As she laid her head against Rytsar's chest, she smiled up at Sir.

Sir wrapped his arm around her, connecting the four of them in a communal hug. Brie hadn't thought she would ever feel this connection again and closed her eyes to soak in the moment.

Just then, Hope made a cute little squeak that caused all three of them to look down at her.

"She has grown much since I left," Rytsar stated with regret.

"She has, old friend," Sir answered, "and we owe that to *you*."

Brie's stomach twisted in a knot, knowing what Sir said was true. They owed Rytsar for saving Hope from a life of childhood slavery.

It scared Brie when she saw the grave look Rytsar

gave Sir, and she pressed herself against the Russian, wanting to meld herself to him. "It's been torture knowing you were in danger."

"*Da*," he answered in a serious tone. "The danger was real, *radost moya*." He turned to look at Titov. "I would not be here if it were not for this man."

Ice ran through Brie's veins hearing how close it had really been. Feeling a profound sense of gratitude, she asked Sir if she could hug Titov.

When Sir nodded, Brie saw tears of gratitude welling up in his own eyes.

Brie handed Hope over to Rytsar, telling him, "This young lady is very grateful to her *dyadya*."

When Rytsar held Hope, however, her eyes grew wide in fear and she began to cry.

"*Nyet, moye solntse*, do not cry. It's your *dyadya*..."

Hope stared fearfully at Rytsar as if he were a stranger, but the moment he began humming his Russian lullaby, Hope's eyes met his and she broke out in a smile. Brie desperately wished she'd had a camera to take a picture of the moment.

Turning away, she walked over to Titov. Unmindful of her tears, she hugged him tightly, thankful beyond words. Letting out a sob, Brie told him, "I will never be able to repay you for everything you've done."

Titov felt extremely stiff in her embrace. Unused to having any physical contact with Brie, he patted her awkwardly in response.

"It was no trouble," he muttered.

She broke away from him, laughing through her tears. "No trouble? You risked your life to save Rytsar because you were protecting our little girl. You are a hero."

It was his turn to laugh. "A hero? No…"

"Yes!" she insisted. "I would do anything to thank you for making this happy reunion possible. Anything."

His face turned beet red. "No need, Mrs. Davis."

"I'm serious. Just name it."

Frowning, he glanced over at Rytsar. "I *do* have one request."

"Yes, anything!" Brie encouraged him.

He looked back at her and said dryly, "Stay out of trouble."

Brie said nothing at first, and then burst out laughing. She had no idea Titov had a sense of humor. No wonder Rytsar had been friends with him for years.

"I promise I'll try," she answered him.

Titov gave her one more awkward pat.

She turned back to Rytsar. "I trust you know what we can do to repay Titov?"

Rytsar stared at the man with a look of profound gratitude. "*Radost moya*, it is not your debt to pay, but mine."

"Brie and I owe you as well, old friend," Sir insisted.

"*Nyet.* You and I are brothers. There is no such thing as a debt between us." Rytsar's gaze moved to Brie, then Hope. "Knowing they're safe is enough."

Watching Rytsar holding their little girl again, Brie wanted to pinch herself. It was hard to believe this was real.

Turning to Sir, she asked, "How long have you known he was coming back?"

He shook his head. "I just found out today." Eying the Russian, he added, "One of us enjoys keeping his closest friends in the dark."

Rytsar gave him an innocent look. "I couldn't stomach disappointing you in case I was delayed."

"That...or your ego demands a grand entrance," Titov muttered.

Sir pointed at Titov, stating, "You hit the nail on the head."

Rytsar smirked, asking him with bravado, "What is the harm in that?"

"But, Rytsar, I've been sick with worry this entire time," Brie protested, glancing at Sir. "We both have."

Still cradling Hope, Rytsar held out an arm to her. "Come."

Brie hesitated a moment, upset that he'd made them suffer longer than necessary, then grumbled, "You're such a sadist."

"*Da*," he agreed with obvious pride. "Now, come to me."

Pouting, Brie reluctantly walked into his embrace. However, she couldn't stay mad at him when she looked down at Hope cradled in his arm.

They were both safe from the slavers because of him.

"You can rest easy, *radost moya*," he assured her in a low voice. "No one is ever going to hurt you or the babe."

She gazed up at Rytsar, the tears threatening to start again. "How can I ever thank you."

"Your beautiful smile is the only thanks I will ever need," he answered.

Brie pressed herself against him, confessing, "I can't quite believe you're back."

His intense gaze held her captive, causing her heart to skip a beat as she stared deep into those blue eyes. She could see that what had happened while he was gone still haunted him, and that he, too, was struggling to believe this was real.

"We're together now. All of us," Brie said, holding her hand out to Sir. "Nothing can break us apart."

The world seemed to stop for a moment as they stood together in silence.

Rytsar finally broke it by stating, "Titov, where's the vodka?"

"The kitchen."

As they made their way into the kitchen, Sir explained to Brie, "Obviously, there is some work to be done in here. While I like the full-sized countertops, I want to replace them with marble."

Brie broke away from him for a moment to run her hands over the extensive counters. "You could feed an army with this much kitchen."

"Among other things," Sir answered her with a private smile.

Brie glanced at the countertops again imagining all the things he had planned and grinned, moving back into his embrace. "I can't wait to officially christen the new counters."

"I bet you can't," Rytsar murmured as he looked knowingly at Sir. "Go ahead, *radost moya*, open the fridge."

Brie walked over and opened the large stainless steel

double-door refrigerator to find a bottle of vodka, four shot glasses, and a jar of pickles inside.

She laughed, taking out the bottle of vodka and handing it to Rytsar. "Would you be kind enough to open it?"

He handed it to Titov. "My friend should do the honors. He is the one who supplied the housewarming gift."

Brie smiled warmly at Titov. "Aww…that's so sweet of you."

Titov cleared his throat, stating, "I understand the importance of vodka in celebrating a welcome home."

Once he opened the bottle, Titov went to pour the first glass, but Brie stopped him.

"No, please. Allow me."

She set the four chilled glasses out, making sure each was a generous pour to express the amount of joy she felt. While she was pouring, Rytsar opened the jar of pickles and held it out so Sir and Titov could each take one.

Brie went to give Sir the first shot to honor him as her Master, but he nodded to Titov instead.

With a grateful smile, Brie gave Titov the first shot glass and silently mouthed the words "thank you" as she handed it to him.

Once everyone had a shot in his or her hand, Sir made the toast. "To this man of valor. May fate reward you many times over."

Titov shook his head at being hailed as a hero but then downed his shot along with everyone else.

Rytsar handed Brie his pickle after she had swallowed the fiery liquid. "Take a bite," he commanded.

She looked at him tenderly as she bit down on the salty, dill goodness.

All of this seems like a dream...

Brie got another round ready for the men, choosing not to partake herself because of the baby.

After a healthy second shot and a hearty shout of "*Za zdarov'ye!*" by all, Rytsar stated, "Your Master must show us around this new beach house."

Brie smiled sheepishly at Sir. "I was so happy to see Rytsar that I forgot there were other rooms in this house."

Sir chuckled warmly. "He is the reason we came tonight. The house, itself"—he looked around the spacious area—"is just the icing on the cake."

Rytsar handed Hope to Sir. "It's only right that her father shows off the new home."

Sir held Hope in his arms, and smiled down at his little girl. "Now the ocean will sing you to sleep every night."

Brie's heart melted when Sir wrapped his other arm around her waist, pulling her close. "This is a new beginning for all of us."

She gazed up at him lovingly. "I can't believe this, Sir."

Looking over at Titov, he said, "Naturally, I want you to join us while we take a tour of the place."

Titov glanced at Rytsar for a moment and then responded with obvious embarrassment, "No, that's unnecessary, Sir Davis."

Sir smirked. "I wasn't asking. We consider you part

of the family now."

Brie nodded enthusiastically.

Titov let out an uncomfortable sigh and glanced at Rytsar again.

Rytsar shrugged. "Better get used to it, Titov. You've earned it."

The man looked back at Sir, nodded curtly and muttered a quick, "Thank you."

Sir slapped him on the back as he gestured to the large room they stood in. "Naturally, this is the great room."

The view of the ocean through the floor to ceiling windows was stunning, but what made the room unique was that the wall was curved in a half-circle, giving the area more room and a more open feel to it.

"I'm in awe, Sir," Brie said, unable to believe this view of the ocean was really theirs to enjoy.

"The arched doorway from the kitchen leads to a formal dining room."

Brie let out a happy squeak as they walked into a large room with its exquisite chair rails, dark wooden floors, and a modern chandelier above. "I've never had a formal dining room before…just think of all the big holiday meals we're going to have in here," she said in wonder.

Sir bounced Hope in his arms. "A lifetime of them."

Brie sighed in contentment. She imagined this room full of family and friends sitting around the table with Sir at the head of it and her sitting beside him.

"On this side of the house," Sir continued, walking down a short hallway. "We have a sizeable office and a guest suite with its own private bathroom."

When Brie saw the guest room, she exclaimed, "If this is the guest room, I can't imagine what the master must look like." She took a peek at the luxurious bathroom attached to the spacious room and whistled in appreciation.

"There's more to this little gem," Sir informed her with a sparkle in his eye. Walking through the bathroom, he opened a door that led outside. "Go ahead. Take a look, babygirl."

As soon as Brie walked through the door, she let out a squeal of delight. "It leads straight to a hot tub?"

Sir chuckled. "Yes. With the ocean in our backyard, I saw no need for a pool. However, I thought a hot tub would be appreciated on cool nights."

Brie looked at the lattice fencing covered in flowering vines that shielded the area from prying beachgoers. "I love the privacy this gives us."

"I do, too," he agreed, leaning down to kiss her. "Anything is possible…"

Rytsar cleared his throat, looking at Titov knowingly.

"Perhaps we should go," Titov suggested.

"Not at all," Rytsar answered, grinning at Brie and Sir. "I'd like to see where this leads."

Sir smirked at Rytsar. "Let me show you the other side of the house."

He led them back through the great room to a set of double doors. Before opening it, he asked, "Any guess what this is, babygirl?"

She grinned. "The place where babies are made?"

He chuckled as the doors swung open dramatically.

"Oh, Sir…this bedroom is huge, and just look at that

view!" Brie walked over to the large windows and stared out at their unobstructed view of the ocean. They were so close that she could see the waves crashing against the shore.

Oh, to make love while looking out at that...

Turning to Sir, she gushed, "This house is amazing in every way."

"The bathroom is nothing to sneeze at, either," Rytsar informed her.

Brie ran over to look and found a tastefully designed Roman-inspired bathroom. White marble steps led up to a Jacuzzi tub with two columns on either side. Colorful Italian tile accented both the tub and the seriously impressive Roman shower.

"I think I could vacation in this bathroom!" she cried.

"It also has an extensive walk-in closet," Sir said, pointing to another door.

Brie kept shaking her head as she explored the multitude of shelves and drawers in the closet. "I can't believe all this is ours."

"There's one other thing unique to this bedroom, and I'm curious what you think about it," Sir told her.

He walked Brie out of the bathroom and over to the other side of the bedroom where she saw another door. Dying to know what was inside, she opened the door and gasped. It was an entire room dedicated to shoes.

"How many shoes did the previous owner have?" she wondered aloud. Twirling in the middle of the giant closet she told him, "This could be Hope's bedroom, it's so big."

Rytsar elbowed Sir in the ribs, chuckling. "You will

have to supply your woman with a lot more shoes, comrade."

Brie walked over to Sir and tweaked Hope's cute little nose. "No matter how many shoes you and I own, sweet pea, I don't think we could *ever* fill up this place."

"Would you like to see the upstairs now?"

She laughed, shaking her head. "I can't believe there's more!"

Repositioning his hold on Hope, Sir wrapped an arm around Brie. "I bought this house with our long-term future in mind."

Brie stood on tiptoes to give him a kiss. "Go ahead, my handsome Master. Show me our future."

The four of them walked up the curved staircase to the second story where there were three more bedrooms and a loft.

Brie was mesmerized by the view of the beach from the loft.

"I was thinking how this would be a perfect office for you," Sir told her.

Brie turned to him, touched beyond words. "You've never given up on my film career."

"No, and neither should you."

Brie wrapped her arms around him, giving him another kiss before leaning down to rub noses with Hope. "You have the most incredible daddy."

Sir showed them the other bedrooms, which were equal in size to each other, along with two separate bathrooms.

"I'll let you decide which room you want to decorate for Hope."

"I hadn't expected Hope would be so far from us,"

Brie said, suddenly concerned.

"It is necessary for two reasons," he explained. "Naturally, I want to preserve our sex life and…" His voice suddenly became somber when he added, "It is safer if she doesn't have a bedroom on the ground level."

Brie nodded, now understanding his concern. There had been a recent story in the news about a child who had been abducted from her bed without her parents being aware of it until the next morning.

After the terrors they'd faced because of Lilly, it only made sense that he'd do whatever he could to protect Hope.

"But, it's so far away from us…" Brie whimpered, looking down the long flight of stairs.

"We'll have a baby monitor with a camera in the room. You won't have to worry about her, Brie, and we can sleep easy knowing she's safe."

Brie nodded, lightly caressing the top of Hope's head. "But not until she's a bit older?"

"Not until you're ready, little mama," Sir assured her.

"Comrade, I noticed there are only three rooms up here. Shouldn't there be five?" Rytsar asked.

Sir chuckled, vehemently shaking his head. "If you are set on five, old friend, have your own damn children."

"*Nyet*," Rytsar replied, putting his arms around Sir and Titov's shoulders. "I am counting on both of you to populate the world."

Titov gave Rytsar an amused side glance.

"As long as you do your duty, I'm not required to,"

Rytsar informed them.

Taking Hope into his arms, he twirled her around, causing her to laugh. "You see, I was made to be a *dyadya*."

Brie adored seeing Rytsar with Hope. Every little girl should know the unconditional love of a *dyadya*.

"I'm so glad you're back!" Brie blurted, unable to contain the joy bursting in her heart.

The smile Rytsar gave her in return made her catch her breath. "There is no place else I would rather be, *radost moya*."

Hope suddenly started squirming in his arms.

He looked down at the babe with concern. "What is wrong, *moye solntse*?"

Brie blushed, feeling the ache in her breasts as her milk came in. "She must be getting hungry."

Rytsar raised an eyebrow. "Ah…then it is time we move this reunion over to my place."

As he headed down the stairs with Hope still cradled in his arms, Brie stood still, wanting to take in the moment.

"Are you okay, babygirl?" Sir asked.

She looked up at him with tears in her eyes. "He's back."

Sir squeezed her hand but said nothing. She understood silence was the only way he could keep control over his emotions.

Brie took his hand and started down the stairs of their new home, smiling at Hope, who was peeking over Rytsar's shoulder.

She couldn't imagine anything cuter.

Joyful Reunion

Titov immediately went to the kitchen to set up more shots when Brie loosened her blouse and undid her bra.

She let out a sigh of relief as Hope began to nurse.

"I missed seeing this," Rytsar murmured to Sir.

"It is a highlight of my day," he answered.

Brie was grateful that both men found the natural act of breastfeeding beautiful and not an act to be hidden.

She loved the connection it gave her with Hope. She'd never experienced anything else like it—that intimate exchange between mother and child—and it was something she deeply cherished.

When Titov came out with four glasses, Brie smiled, grateful to him for including her. After the evening feeding, Hope normally slept through the night, and Brie had extra milk stored for occasions such as this.

While she finished nursing, Brie insisted the men take another shot together. She enjoyed the open talk and intimacy that vodka seemed to bring out in both Sir and Rytsar. She was positive they had volumes to say to each other.

Instead of getting emotional, however, the men started ribbing each other. When Titov threw in a few embarrassing moments involving Rytsar, he soon had Brie laughing so hard that she accidentally broke the suction with Hope and her nipple popped out.

Apologizing to her little girl, she quickly helped Hope latch on and then glanced up to see Sir and Rytsar staring at her. She noticed their looks changing from ones of admiration to longing.

She needed that connection with them as well and blushed under their dual attention.

After Hope had finished, Brie turned her over and gently rubbed her back until she let out a healthy burp, which incited a round of proud applause from the three men.

Grinning, Brie looked over at Titov. She was again hit with a deep sense of gratitude.

"Would you like to hold her?" she asked.

He shook his head vigorously. "I'm no good with children."

"Nonsense," Rytsar stated. "Hold her."

Titov scoffed.

"Did you not risk your life to save her in Tatianna's name?"

Brie saw a flicker of pain in Titov's eyes at the mention of his sister.

"Hold her," Rytsar insisted.

Titov sat down next to Brie and looked at her dubiously as he held out his arms. Brie carefully laid the baby in his arms. Hope stared up at Titov with curiosity and a milk-dazed smile.

"She is so…perfect," he said, staring down at her.

Brie was touched by his reaction to her daughter. When Hope's eyelids became heavy and she grew sleepy, Brie smiled. "She's safe tonight because of you."

Titov continued to stare at Hope with a far-off look, tears slowly rolling down his cheeks. Brie suspected that he was thinking about his little sister. Brie hoped that his knowing that he had saved their daughter from a similar fate gave him some peace.

"Would you like me to take her?" Brie asked after several minutes.

At first, she didn't think he'd heard her until he answered, "No. She looks so peaceful."

Sir smiled, gazing down at Hope. "Yes, holding a sleeping child does have a calming effect I've never appreciated until now."

"I am content to hold her," Titov told Brie. Looking down at Hope, he added, "I couldn't save Tatianna, but…"

"You saved this little one," Rytsar said, clasping his shoulder. "And me."

Titov glanced up at him. "I could do no less."

Rytsar shook his head. "*Nyet.* You could have run to save yourself and left me to my fate."

"Your fate *is* my fate."

Titov looked back at Hope lying in his arms, gazing at her with a look of puzzled wonderment. "Just as this little girl is tied to Tatianna now."

Rytsar nodded, looking down at the baby with tears

in his eyes. "*Da*, this little one ties all of us together. Her happiness will be our happiness."

The three of them nodded in agreement.

Titov glanced up at them standing there and said, "Now leave me, so I can hold this child in peace."

Rytsar nodded, putting his hand around the back of Brie's neck, giving her chills. Turning to Sir he asked, "Shall we?"

Brie's heart skipped a beat when she felt Sir's hand on the small of her back.

The dominant hold each man had on her as he led her to the bedroom, caused her heart to race.

Once the bedroom doors were closed, they showered her with kisses. These weren't the kisses of demanding Dominants, but the passionate kisses of long-lost lovers.

"You undress her," Sir murmured in a gruff voice, as his lips moved from her neck to her mouth.

Brie felt a gush of wetness as Rytsar pulled at the button of her pants and unzipped them.

"It has been too long, *radost moya*," he growled as he pulled them down and his hand stroked her pussy.

Sir continued his deep kisses, his tongue exploring her mouth, while Rytsar made quick work of her clothing.

Brie moaned into Sir's mouth when she felt Rytsar rub her wet clit, teasing it with his skilled fingers.

"Let's take her to the bed," Rytsar muttered lustfully.

Brie squeaked in excitement when Sir swept her up in his arms and carried her to the bed, placing her gently on it.

She lay there completely naked, staring up at Rytsar and Sir. "I want you both to lie with me," she begged, holding her hands out to them.

Rytsar looked at her, his eyes smoldering with desire as both men began undressing.

"*Radost moya...*"

Her pet name rolled off his lips like a love song.

Brie's eyes trailed over him. She admired his muscular body covered in scars and his signature dragon tattoo. Then, suddenly, her breath caught.

She stared at the tattoo she knew so well, noticing that Rytsar had made an addition to it that she'd never seen before. The dragon now had smoke swirling from its mouth and over his chest and heart. Within those swirls were cleverly designed letters that spelled out the words *"radost moya"*.

Brie met his gaze, tears welling in her eyes.

He lay down beside her and reached out, stroking her cheek gently. "No tears, *radost moya*."

Brie glanced at Sir and could see he was equally affected.

"Before I went into battle, I covered myself in armor," Rytsar explained.

Opening his hand, he showed her a stylized sun that had been tattooed in the palm of his hand. "I wanted *moye solntse* with me when I made the final blow."

Brie swallowed hard, tears coming to her eyes as she traced the outline of the sun with her finger.

Sir joined them on the bed, pressing himself against Brie. "I will be forever grateful you survived that battle, brother."

Rytsar placed his hand over his heart. "I was protected."

Brie opened her mouth to say something, but Rytsar gazed deep into her eyes and commanded, "No more talk."

"Let your men make love to you," Sir said, moving down between her legs while Rytsar claimed her lips.

Brie floated in a haze of sexual bliss as they pleased and teased her body as only these two men could, taking her on both an emotional and physical high.

When she got to the edge, teetering on the verge of climax, Sir changed positions. Lying on his back, he nodded to Rytsar, who pulled a tube of lubricant from his nightstand and threw it to Sir.

Before he covered his shaft in lubricant, Brie asked, "May I kiss your cock, Master?"

He lay the tube down and smiled, nodding.

Brie gave the head of his shaft a chaste kiss before taking a lick of his precome. She smiled, then opened her mouth and encased the head of his cock with her warm lips.

Sir groaned in pleasure as she slowly took in his length.

Reaching out with her hand, Brie grasped Rytsar's hard shaft and began stroking him with the same rhythm as she was sucking Sir.

Brie felt a thrill when she tasted more of Sir's precome. It let her know how much he was enjoying her mouth. Sucking even harder, she was gratified when Sir groaned again.

It sent chills of electricity straight to her groin, making her pussy ache in need.

Breaking her oral embrace with Sir, she turned her attention on Rytsar, while still pleasing Sir with her hand.

Rytsar let out a low, primal growl as his shaft disappeared into her mouth. Grabbing the back of her head, he guided her to take him deeper. She consciously relaxed her throat and was rewarded with his manly groan of satisfaction.

Brie swirled her tongue along the ridge of his shaft when he released her, treating it like a lollypop. As a finishing touch, she looked up at the Russian and smiled before kissing the tip tenderly.

When she heard Sir applying a liberal amount of lubricant to his shaft, she turned her head to watch. Her pussy gushed with wetness at the thought of being taken by both men at the same time.

Brie was entranced as she watched Sir stroke his cock, covering it in the lubricant. When he was satisfied, he held up his hand and Rytsar threw him a hand towel. Once clean, he tossed it to the floor and turned to Brie.

"Impale yourself on me."

Brie bit her lip as she moved into the reverse cowgirl position, her pussy hovering just above his hard cock. Lowering herself down slowly, Brie guided the head of his shaft into her tight ass, pressing against it.

Brie let out a little gasp as his shaft opened her up, breaching her tight entrance as the entirety of the head slipped inside her.

"That's it, babygirl," Sir growled in a low, seductive voice, grabbing her waist to help her farther down his cock.

Once he was deep enough to change positions, Brie used his body to support herself as she moved her legs forward and laid down, her back against his chest.

Sir wrapped his arms around her and nuzzled her neck. Like his kisses, he was sensual and loving as he pushed his cock into her, murmuring about how much he enjoyed fucking her ass.

Brie smiled, leaning her head back to give in to the delicious sensation of his hard cock stroking her from the inside. "I've always loved it when you take me like this."

Rytsar reached out and grasped her left breast, squeezing it firmly. "So suckable," he whispered hoarsely. The warmth of his mouth encased her nipple as his tongue swirled around it before he began sucking hard.

Brie moaned with pleasure as Rytsar worshipped her breast with his mouth while Sir slowly thrust his shaft into her ass.

This was sexual bliss—every lick, suck, and stroke.

Eventually, Rytsar moved into position, needing more.

Brie looked up at him, feeling deliciously vulnerable as he spread her legs wide.

He gazed at her pussy while he stroked his cock with his hand. "I do not want to rush this," he murmured huskily as he pressed his cock against her swollen pussy.

The changes in Rytsar made her feel uncertain. Normally, he was demanding when the three of them scened together, but tonight he seemed subdued—different, somehow.

Brie bit her bottom lip as he pushed his cock into

her. Even though she had taken Rytsar this way numerous times, it still required her body to relax and submit to their double penetration.

It was part of the reason she enjoyed it so much. The act always challenged her, and the connection it created between them was like nothing else she had experienced.

Sir gauged his thrusts to coincide with Rytsar's as the two men started moving together.

When Brie gazed up into Rytsar's blue eyes, her heart skipped a beat.

He was staring at her sadly as if he'd already lost her and was making love to a ghost.

The sight of the tears welling up in his eyes overwhelmed her. Rytsar wasn't a man to cry.

Seeing his reaction, Brie suddenly realized how truly close it had been.

Rytsar never expected to come back…

Even now, with his shaft deep inside her, he was struggling to believe this was real. Brie knew that and it broke her heart.

Tears rolled down her cheeks as they made love, her body rocked by the gentle movements of both men.

Afterward, when Rytsar went to disengage, she wrapped her arms tightly around him and whispered, "You're back."

Positioning herself between both men, Brie savored the afterglow of the scene, as the three lay silently on the bed.

She eventually broke the silence by asking the question that had been burning a hole in her heart all night. "What happened, Rytsar?"

Brie could feel Rytsar shaking his head on the pillow.

She turned to lie on her stomach so she could face him. "I need to know."

He shook his head again. "*Nyet.*"

"Please…"

He would not look at her. Instead, he stared up at the ceiling.

"You cannot imagine what we have seen, the horrors we were subjected to. Titov and I have been permanently scarred by it."

Turning his head toward her, he added in a grave tone. "If I were to speak them aloud, you would not be able to forget it. It would eat at you as it does me."

She smiled sadly when his rough hand grazed her cheek.

"I don't want you to be haunted by it as I am, *radost moya.*"

"But—" she began to protest, wanting to carry his burden.

Sir interrupted, commanding gently, "Trust him, babygirl."

Brie nodded and laid her head on Rytsar's chest as she reached for Sir's hand. She felt a sense of contentment when Sir took her hand and squeezed it, while she listened to Rytsar's steady heartbeat.

She had to believe he would recover from this now that the three of them were together.

Love was a mysterious force of great power.

A Night with the Gallants

Brie was busy packing up the nonessentials in the apartment in anticipation of the move. She'd started with all of her college stuff, which she had failed to sift through before.

Among the many treasures she'd discovered during the culling was a little beat-up, yellow handbook that she had carried with her through all four years of college. It was titled simply *The Essentials of Filmmaking*.

She held it up for Hope to see. "I know this doesn't look important, but this little paperback meant the world to me in college." Flipping through the pages, she murmured to herself, "It still does…"

One of Brie's teachers had given her the small book on the day of her high school graduation. Looking over at Hope, who was watching her from her carrier, she said, "Miss Fushimi gave me this."

Brie smiled, thinking back on her high school teacher. She had been recording short films about her family and the small town she'd grown up in for years, but it wasn't until Miss Fushimi came into her life that anyone had taken her seriously.

"Do you know what she said when she gave this to me?" Brie asked Hope, waving the paperback in the air.

Hope bounced in her carrier, holding her hands up, wanting to grab it.

Brie laughed, loving her daughter's enthusiasm and curiosity.

"Miss Fushimi told me, 'Everything you need to know is in this book.' She said it with such confidence that I believed her."

She looked through the pages again with fondness. "And this little book really did have a fountain of good advice."

She glanced at Hope. "But it wasn't what was printed in it that made this important to me..." Opening it up to the title page, Brie held it up to show her. "It was the message Miss Fushimi wrote inside it."

Brie stared down at her teacher's beautiful handwriting and smiled as she read the words aloud:

Follow your heart, Brianna Bennett, and you are guaranteed success.

Brie traced her fingers over the handwritten words, a lump growing in her throat. "Everyone questioned my plans to become a filmmaker—except her. She was the one who gave me the courage to head out to LA on my own to get my film degree."

Looking back down at the writing again, Brie was overcome with a sense of profound sadness. "Miss Fushimi will never know the difference she made to me."

A tear slowly rolled down Brie's cheek as she told Hope, "That amazing woman died of breast cancer three years after she gave this to me." She wiped away the tear, telling her daughter. "But her words still live on in—"

"I guess I owe Miss Fushimi a debt of gratitude, then," Sir said from the doorway.

Brie turned to him, nodding with a sad smile.

"Hand it to me and I will pack it with your personal items. We don't want it getting lost."

"Thank you, Sir."

As she was handing him the book, Sir mentioned, "I just got a call from the Gallants. We've been asked to join them for dinner tonight."

She was thrilled to hear they would be visiting Mr. Gallant and his wife, Ena, so she made quick work of the rest of the box, wanting to get ready.

Brie hadn't seen either of them since throwing the adoption party for the Reynolds at Rytsar's beach house. She cherished any time spent with the Gallants because she held both of them in the highest esteem.

Later that evening, when they arrived at the Gallants' house, Ena answered the door and greeted them warmly. "It is lovely to see you again, Sir Davis."

She gave him a slight bow of her head before turning to Brie and smiling. "I can't believe how much Hope has grown already."

Brie looked down at their little girl, who was staring

at Ena with big doe eyes, obviously smitten with the tall, exotic woman.

When Ena leaned down and made cute baby noises, Hope graced her with an adorable smile.

"She is absolutely precious," Ena told Brie, her eyes sparkling.

Mr. Gallant came up from behind and placed his hand in the small of his wife's back. Brie had always loved the contrast between the couple. Mr. Gallant was a tiny man with pale skin, and Ena, an unusually tall woman, with a radiant dark complexion.

Despite their height difference, there was no mistaking that he was a Dominant. An authoritative confidence emanated from the man.

Mr. Gallant took one look at Hope, turned to Sir, and stated good-humoredly, "You're in trouble, Sir Davis. That little girl of yours is going to have a line of boyfriends out the door. Mark my words."

Sir chuckled. "Luckily, I'll be able to learn from your experience before Hope hits that age."

Mr. Gallant sighed heavily. "It's already starting for me. Kalisha is only fifteen, not even old enough to date yet, but I have to fend the boys off constantly."

Brie laughed. "Well, I'm not surprised, Mr. Gallant. You have two beautiful daughters."

Mr. Gallant frowned good-naturedly, looking at Sir. "It is a father's curse."

He then turned to his wife. "But, it's one I willingly accept because I'm lucky my girls take after their mother."

"We will survive this together, husband," Ena assured him.

Mr. Gallant took her hand and kissed it. "Yes, we will." He looked at her with such admiration and tenderness that it made Brie's heart melt.

Turning back to them, Mr. Gallant apologized. "How rude of me to stand here talking in the doorway. Please, do come in."

Sir gestured for Brie to go first with the baby and gave Hope a wink as they passed by. Brie loved little interactions like that between Sir and Hope. Their daughter definitely seemed to bring out Sir's lighter side.

Brie turned her head and smiled back at Sir as they walked down the hallway. He'd been afraid he would be too distant to be a good father, but what he hadn't realized was the influence his daughter would have over him. There was nothing he wouldn't do for his little girl...

Ena led them to a room where Captain, Candy, and Baron were already seated. She bowed her head slightly, stating, "I must take care of the finishing touches for the meal."

"Can I do anything to help?" Brie offered.

"No, my daughters enjoy helping me with dinner. Please stay and visit with the others."

As she left the room, Baron stood up and walked over to Brie. "So, this is the little one?" He hadn't been able to attend the large gathering at Rytsar's and had yet to see their baby.

"Would you like to hold her?" Brie asked.

He grinned uncomfortably. "I don't know how, really. Better pass."

"I would love for Hope to get to know you better," she told him. She helped rest Hope's small head in his strong arms and smiled up at him. "Luckily, she doesn't break."

Baron's arms were noticeably stiff as he looked down at the baby, but Brie saw him slowly starting to relax as he continued to hold her.

"She's so tiny."

Brie giggled. "Actually, she's growing like a weed. You should have seen her when she was born."

Kissing Hope's little hand, she told him. "She was such a tiny thing back then."

"I can't even imagine," Baron stated. "But I have to say, she definitely takes after her mother."

Hope held up her hands, wanting to touch Baron's face. He obliged her and chuckled when Hope tickled his chin with her small fingers. "She is a cute little thing."

"I knew she would like you, Baron." Brie smiled. "Like mother, like daughter…"

"Are the two of you planning to make more?" he asked, raising an eyebrow.

Her cheeks reddened as she glanced at Sir. "Actually, we are."

"We believe every child deserves a sibling," Sir stated. "Someone to share their childhood with."

Baron laughed. "Well, I have to agree with that. Life wouldn't be the same without brothers and sisters."

He looked over at Captain questioningly before asking Sir, "Does that mean we will have to wait a few more years before you are able to join us?"

Sir glanced at Brie.

"We have talked about it," he answered slowly. "Would you be open to us doing isolated lessons rather than being on staff? It would give us a chance to gauge how effective our lessons are and if this is something that will work for us in the future."

Baron looked to Captain and Candy, who both nodded their approval.

Giving Hope back to Brie, he held out his hand to Sir. "I think that is a fine idea, Sir Davis."

Sir smiled, shaking Baron's hand firmly. "Fortunately, Hope is at an age now where we feel comfortable leaving her with others. So, until Brie is pregnant again and can no longer work alongside me, we will commit what time we can to your program."

"That's wonderful!" Candy cried, smiling at Brie.

Captain got up and walked over to them, first shaking Sir's hand and then Brie's. "This is excellent news. Excellent! I look forward to observing your lessons with our students."

Brie's stomach jumped a little at the thought of Captain observing them. It was silly since she'd grown used to being critiqued as a student at the Center and was an experienced sub now.

How funny that she was even worried…

With Sir as her partner, she had no reason to feel anxious. He had proven that when they had scened in front of the sadists in Russia, at a time when she was still relatively new to the lifestyle.

"No one else in the room matters…"

Sir had told her that then, and it held true even now.

Brie looked at her Master with confidence. "With Sir

leading the demonstration, I am certain it will be a success."

"I, for one, am glad to hear that you will be taking on a teaching role again, Sir Davis," Mr. Gallant said. "You have a natural predisposition for it."

Sir inclined his head to him. "Coming from you, Gallant, I appreciate that."

Mr. Gallant's oldest daughter stepped into the room, announcing, "Dinner is almost ready."

He smiled proudly. "Thank you, Kalisha."

As they all made their way into the formal dining room, Brie saw Nyah was almost finished setting the table. The child was so precise in the placement of each piece of silverware that Brie found it endearing.

"What a lovely table," she complimented the girl.

Nyah grinned at her. "Thank you, Mrs. Davis. I like it to look perfect for our guests."

When they were all seated, Ena came out with a large tray of prime rib roast, which she gracefully set down next to Mr. Gallant.

The roast was huge!

Kalisha followed behind her mother, carrying a bowl of whipped potatoes.

Ena stated proudly, "Kalisha made the potatoes herself." She looked at Mr. Gallant proudly. "I think they are her best yet, husband."

Smiling, he looked over at his daughter. "I can't wait to taste them."

Kalisha beamed at her father as she set the bowl on the table and took her seat.

Mr. Gallant picked up the carving knife and began

slicing the roast.

"I felt a special dinner was in order," Mr. Gallant stated once he'd finished cutting the meat. He looked at each person sitting at the table. "To call such quality people our friends seems a good reason to celebrate."

Each piece of prime rib practically filled up a plate by itself. When Ena handed Brie hers, Brie stared at it, silently wondering how she could possibly finish all of it.

"Don't worry about eating it all, Mrs. Davis," Ena assured her.

Brie heard Candy let out a breath of relief and glanced over at her, smiling knowingly. There was no way either of them could finish even half of it.

"If you have any scraps left over, we'll be happy to take them home to our dogs. I know they will appreciate it," Captain told Mr. Gallant.

"Wonderful," he answered. "I hate to see good meat go to waste."

Brie picked up her fork and went for the potatoes Kalisha made first. They were surprisingly smooth and creamy, with just the right seasoning to complement the steak. "Kalisha, these potatoes are amazing! I never knew mashed potatoes could be so light and creamy."

Kalisha smiled. "Thank you, Mrs. Davis. My secret is pressing them through the potato ricer several times to get that smooth texture."

"Sounds like a lot of work," Brie replied, taking another forkful. "But it definitely seems worth it. Delicious!"

The table suddenly became silent while everyone enjoyed the extravagant meal.

After several minutes, Nyah spoke up. "Do you have pictures of your newest dog, Captain?"

"We sure do," Candy answered, digging through her purse for her phone. She passed it to Nyah. "Here is our newest fur baby."

"Aww...she's so cute!" Nyah cooed, passing the phone to Brie so she could see.

"The big one is Rosko and the small one is Annie," Candy explained.

Brie immediately noticed both dogs had the telltale signs of gray around their eyes. "How old are your pups?"

"They're both seniors," Candy answered, looking over at Captain. "We feel like that's our calling. Giving older dogs that no one wants happiness at the end of their lives is important to both of us.

Brie brought her hand to her chest, exclaiming, "Oh, my goodness. That's so wonderful!"

Captain grunted, his expression somber. "Most dogs with any hint of gray get euthanized because everyone is looking for a puppy. The older dogs don't stand a chance."

"That's so sad..." Brie said.

"It is because most of these older dogs have been left behind because of the owner's death or the family having to relocate. These poor dogs have no idea what they've done wrong and their hearts are broken."

Candy looked at Captain tenderly. "I love that Captain has vowed to keep adopting them."

He smiled at his pet. "It's a simple way for the two of us to make a positive difference in the world."

"Well, I think it's wonderful!" Brie exclaimed as she handed the phone to Sir.

Brie saw Mr. Gallant take Ena's hand and kiss it at the end of the meal. She had noticed he'd done something similar halfway through the meal when he had reached out and squeezed her hand.

Both times, Ena had looked into his eyes and smiled. It was so incredibly sweet.

"Girls," Mr. Gallant said, addressing his daughters. "It's time to clear the table, but don't bother doing the dishes tonight. Your mother and I will attend to them later. Since our meal has run later than usual, I want to make sure you have plenty of time to finish your homework."

After the table was cleared, both girls headed upstairs.

Brie shook her head in disbelief. "You've done such a wonderful job with your children. They really pitched in tonight and seemed genuinely happy to help with the meal."

Ena smiled. "Since they were little, we've stressed how important each member is to the well-being of our family. It's something we all take seriously."

When Hope began to fuss, Sir got up and brought her to the table. Now that Kalisha and Nyah were gone, Brie felt comfortable to be more open.

Looking at Hope sitting on his knee, she confessed, "Raising a child as a practicing D/s couple is easy at Hope's age, but I'll admit I'm concerned about carving out that time for Sir when she's older. Like you, we want Hope to decide on her sexual preferences based on her own needs and desires, and not because she's grown up aware that we're in the lifestyle."

Mr. Gallant sat back in his chair and nodded. "While your children *must* come first, it is imperative that a D/s couple set time aside daily to keep their relationship vibrant and healthy."

"But how can you do it without your girls figuring it out? Especially as they get older?"

"We planned things out when they were young by setting up a strict schedule in our home. To the outside world, and to our girls, it seems completely normal. They head upstairs for homework at eight and need to be in bed by nine. By ten o'clock, we're free to reconnect with each other."

"How do you keep your toys hidden when children are naturally curious?" Baron asked, clearly intrigued.

"Let me show you," Mr. Gallant said. He stood up, inviting them to follow.

As was his habit, he placed his hand on the small of Ena's back as they walked up the stairs, but Brie noticed that Mr. Gallant pressed two of his fingers against her back rather than his entire palm.

At the top of the stairs, Ena nodded to Mr. Gallant before telling us, "Please excuse me while I check on the girls."

Mr. Gallant led them to their bedroom and, once everyone was inside, shut the door, explaining, "Since the girls would think it strange to have all of our guests enter our bedroom, I had Ena check on them to make sure they are preoccupied."

"Won't they be able to hear us talking?" Captain

asked.

"Actually, to aid them with their studies and help them to sleep, we have classical music set at a low level in both of their rooms. Not only does it have an overall calming effect, but it also lessens the chance of our girls overhearing us while we play."

Ena opened the door and quietly entered the room. "They are both focused on their homework and wanted to thank you again for doing their dishes, Husband."

Mr. Gallant's eyes twinkled as he nodded in acknowledgment. "I was just telling our friends how we ensure the girls are not disturbed by our nightly encounters."

Ena's laugh was gentle and sweet. "I never knew how much a gag can become a submissive's best friend."

Brie glanced at Sir and winked.

"As far as our toys…" Mr. Gallant stated, resting his hands on the oak countertop of their wet bar. "…you are right, Baron. Humans are naturally curious. I cannot fault my children for that. Rather than take chances, I had this wet bar built in the bedroom." He patted the varnished oak with fondness. "My daughters think that their mother and father enjoy a nightcap in bed each evening, so it only makes sense that the bar is locked. No one would question it."

He fished out a key from under his shirt, which was attached to a silver chain around his neck. "There is only one key and I never take it off."

Mr. Gallant leaned down to unlock a center lock and Brie heard multiple locks sliding back at the same time.

"One key unlocks them all," he explained as he

opened all of the wooden doors, exposing a wealth of BDSM tools, including a colorful selection of wax.

Mr. Gallant glanced at Brie. "Naturally, there is always the possibility that despite our strict bedtime schedule and the classical music, the girls might need one of us. So, to prevent them from walking in unannounced, we have made locking the bedroom door the first of our nightly rituals."

Ena nodded, smiling as she confided, "Because of our nightly ritual, I must admit that whenever I hear a door lock now, my body instantly responds regardless of where I am."

Candy giggled. "I can only imagine."

"Similar to Pavlov's dog?" Brie asked, grinning.

"Yes," Ena chuckled lightly. She looked at Mr. Gallant. "But I wouldn't change a thing. I appreciate that our girls are protected from accidental exposure, and I am well cared for as a submissive."

"I have to hand it to you, Gallant. It appears you thought of everything," Baron said.

Mr. Gallant took Ena's hand and squeezed it as he told Baron, "My family is the most important thing to me."

Charmed by Mr. Gallant's many gestures toward his wife, Brie suddenly realized what they were really about.

"Mr. Gallant, when you squeeze Ena's hand, does that mean something?"

He smiled at her, clearly impressed that she had noticed. "It does, Mrs. Davis. I believe the best way to maintain a healthy D/s in public is to constantly acknowledge my wife's submission. What better way to express that than a simple squeeze of the hand to let her know I see and value her submission."

Brie loved his answer.

"A brilliant way to handle it," Sir stated.

"My husband is exceptional as a Dominant," Ena said with pride.

Mr. Gallant took Ena's hand and kissed it, looking deeply into her eyes.

"I've seen you do that several times tonight, Mr. Gallant. Does it also have a meaning?" Candy asked.

Ena answered for him, not breaking eye contact with her husband, "It means 'I am well pleased.'"

Both Brie and Candy murmured "aww" under their breath at the same time and then looked at each other and giggled.

Nothing makes a sub happier than to hear their Master is pleased…

Brie was certain when she saw Mr. Gallant pressing two fingers against his wife's back that it meant something, too. "What about when you two were heading up the stairs?"

Mr. Gallant smiled kindly. "You are very observant, Mrs. Davis, but that is something we will keep to ourselves."

Brie nodded, feeling slightly embarrassed that she'd asked.

"No need to feel ashamed for asking, Mrs. Davis," Mr. Gallant assured her, easily reading the expression on her face.

Turning to Sir, he explained, "I believe it is important for each couple to establish their own silent signals. It prevents us from all doing the same thing and exposing ourselves to possible discovery."

"Very astute," Sir agreed.

It relieved Brie to know it was possible to continue their twenty-four seven relationship even as Hope was growing up. Plus, the prospect of coming up with a secret language only Sir and she knew would be so exciting!

"Thank you for sharing so much with us, Mr. Gallant. Even though I'm no longer a student in your class, you still continue to teach me," Brie gushed.

He nodded to her. "It is my sincere pleasure, Mrs. Davis."

At the end of the evening, once they made it back home, Brie let out a happy sigh. "This was a wonderful night, Sir."

"I agree."

"I'm so glad Baron, Captain, and Candy were there. It's a dream come true for me that you'll be training again."

He put an arm around her. "But this time around, you are going to be by my side."

Brie stared at him, a feeling of joy washing over her. *How did I get so lucky?*

Weekend Retreat

Sir walked into the room where Brie was busy packing. "Babygirl, I'm going to postpone the move temporarily. Besides the countertops, there is an additional change I'd like to make to personalize our home."

Brie's curiosity piqued, she put down the vase she'd been wrapping. "What kind of change, Sir?"

"It's a surprise."

She raised her eyebrows. "But you know I'm no good with surprises…"

"Exactly," he said with a charming smirk. "You still lack patience, my little sub. As your Master, it is my solemn duty to assist in your growth in that area."

Brie *almost* rolled her eyes but, thankfully, didn't.

However, Sir was looking at her as if he knew she wanted to. Blushing under his intense scrutiny, she chose to change the subject. "Should I keep packing then?"

"No, while we wait for the contractors to finish, I'd like you to revisit your film projects and decide which one you would like to release next."

"Yes, Sir," Brie answered dutifully, then let out a heavy sigh. "I really want to get started filming the documentary about your father and his beloved violin…" She groaned, locked in her indecision.

"But I have all the scenes filmed for that second documentary. It would be easy to finish it, and Mary insists she can help get it released. However, I don't really want to work with Mr. Holloway again—not after the way he treated Faelan and Mary."

Sir looked at her thoughtfully. "I encourage you to go over the material you have accumulated for both films. It should help give you some clarity. Your choice should come from the project you feel most passionate about."

The smile he gave her made her feel cherished. "I see no reason for you to put off your film career any longer, now that I am recovered and Durov has returned to us."

Brie broke out in a huge smile, still amazed by their good fortune.

"Yes, you are almost fully recovered, and Rytsar won't have any reason to leave us again. On top of that, we have a beautiful new home on the beach." She shook her head in amazement. "To think where we were and where we are now…it's a miracle."

"A miracle, yes. However, it's also proof that one should never give up."

"True," she said, wrapping her arms around him. "We'll never give up because we're condors."

Sir leaned down to kiss the top of her head. "Condors forever, babygirl."

Brie let out a contented sigh. "I'm so happy right

now."

"I know how I can make you even happier."

She looked at him with a flirtatious smile. "I bet you do, Sir."

Closing her eyes in anticipation as he leaned in for a kiss, Brie could feel his lips just centimeters from hers. Instead of kissing her, he said, "I want you to pack a bag for the weekend."

Her eyes popped open. "Where are we going?"

"Durov has invited us to stay at his place for the weekend while I go over my new plans with the contractors."

Brie's eyes lit up. "Oh, I can't think of a better way to spend the weekend."

Sir nodded his agreement. "It'll give the three of us the time we need."

"And Rytsar will get his *dyadya* time with Hope."

"Yes, and that is important, as well."

She looked at him playfully. "I can't believe you teased me with that almost kiss just now."

He raised an eyebrow. "Has it left you needy?"

"Yes, Sir."

"What would you like?"

"I would like a kiss, Sir."

"Beg for it, babygirl," he commanded seductively.

Brie tilted her head up and looked into Sir's eyes with genuine desire. "Please, Sir. I'm begging you for a kiss."

No sooner were the words out of her mouth than she felt his firm lips pressed against hers. The man still had the ability to take her breath away with a simple kiss and she melted against him.

When he released her, Brie let out a little gasp.

"You'll receive another once you're done packing your bag."

Brie felt butterflies in her stomach as she turned to leave. She traced her fingers over her tingling lips while she walked down the hall.

Going to the baby's room first, she started to pack for the weekend. She smiled to herself as she folded Hope's tiny clothes in the suitcase.

To honor Sir's wishes, Brie also packed up her laptop to bring with her. She wanted to look over all the scenes she had already filmed.

Now that Hope was six months old, Brie could pretty much take her anywhere she needed to go. There was no reason why being a mother should hinder her film career.

"*Radost moya*, it is good to see you again!" Rytsar said, answering the door with exaggerated enthusiasm.

"What? No greeting for me?" Sir mumbled.

"Eh…" The Russian looked at him as if unimpressed. "Greetings, peasant."

Brie giggled. "We know the only reason you invited the two of us was to see Hope."

Rytsar put his hand over his heart and looked properly wounded. He then proceeded to whisk Hope from her arms.

"Let me show you your new room, *moye solntse*."

Brie glanced at Sir before following Rytsar down the hallway to one of his guest rooms. She was touched when she saw the plaque on the door. It was a colorful sun that resembled the one tattooed on his palm, and it had the words "moye solntse" written around the center of it.

"That's so sweet, Rytsar," she cooed, tracing the words around the sun.

"You haven't seen anything yet," he stated proudly as he opened the door.

Brie's jaw dropped when she stepped inside with Sir beside her. The first thing she spotted was a crib with a canopy of white silk. To the right of the crib was a huge white dresser that was taller than Brie.

Curious, she asked if she could open a drawer.

"But of course," Rytsar answered, gesturing to it.

Brie walked over and pulled out a middle drawer. Inside were a variety of frilly dresses separated by color. Brie shook her head as she opened another drawer. It had an array of tiny bathing suits.

"What have you done, bought out a whole store?" she teased.

"I want *moye solntse* to have whatever she needs when she visits me."

"We're only going to be a few houses down," Brie laughed.

Sir nodded to the left side of the room. "What's with the horse?"

Brie turned to see a replica of a miniature pony set on wooden rockers. It looked real, from its black and white fur and long mane, to its soft brown eyes with long lashes.

"Every young lady needs a horse, and I didn't want *moye solntse* lacking for one until she is old enough to own a real one."

Sir shook his head, but it was obvious that Hope was entranced by the miniature pony by the way she reached out for the horse and then looked up at Rytsar pleadingly. He walked over to it, giving Sir a smug expression as Hope grabbed the mane with both hands and squealed in delight.

"You're incorrigible," Sir muttered.

"I'm the *dyadya*, it's my right."

Brie smiled. "But, Rytsar, you promised you weren't going to spoil her."

"This is not spoiling," he insisted, glancing around the room. "If you knew what I wanted to get her, you would understand that I've shown the greatest restraint."

Brie glanced over at Sir, who had a bemused expression on his face.

Rytsar pointed. "Did you see that I set up a comfortable area for you to nurse her, *radost moya*?"

She looked in the corner of the room he was pointing to and saw a rocking chair with intricate flower designs covering it. Beside it was a small table with a lampshade with the same flowery pattern. He walked over and opened the little table drawer. "I have only the best treats should you get hungry while you nurse."

Brie shook her head, stunned when she looked inside. There were little pretty packages of nuts, dried fruit, a yummy looking confection labeled a lactation cookie, and dark chocolates with raspberry.

"And I even bought the most advanced breast pump on the market so there's no need to worry about bringing your own, should you have need of one."

Grinning, he picked up a remote on the little table. "As far as sleep time? *Moye solntse* will drift into dreamland to only the finest music." He clicked the remote and the lights in the room dimmed as tiny stars lit up the ceiling and a soft sonata played in the background.

"She is guaranteed sweet dreams when she is here."

When Rytsar turned the lights back up, Brie glanced around the room again, noting that he had supplied it with every baby convenience known to man. "You don't think this is overkill, even for a *dyadya*?"

"Not at all," he assured her.

When Hope started to fuss, Sir chided, "It's far too much. You've overwhelmed our little girl."

"*Nyet.*" Rytsar looked at Brie knowingly. "She's simply hungry."

Brie smiled to herself because he was right. "It's true. Hope normally nurses at this time and then goes down for her afternoon nap."

Rytsar handed the baby over to Brie, then showed her how to work the remote for the lights and the music, reminding Brie to partake of the plentiful snacks. He then turned to Sir and clasped him on the shoulder.

"Let us leave mother and child to bond in *moye solntse*'s new room while we lay out on the beach. There are things you and I must discuss."

Brie looked at Sir, who nodded his approval. "Come join us when you're done. I'll have a bikini laid out for you to wear."

After the men left, Brie sat down in the rocking chair with Hope. It was actually a relief to finally nurse because her breasts were starting to ache. It amazed Brie that her body knew Hope's schedule so well and provided her with exactly what her baby needed.

After she settled into the chair, she let out a soft moan. The rocking chair was the most comfortable one she'd ever sat in. It felt as if it had been made especially for her—which it probably had.

Brie slowly rocked Hope as she fed her, looking down at her little girl. "You have a crazy uncle."

Reaching over without disturbing Hope, Brie pulled the little drawer open. Picking up one of the chocolates, she unwrapped it and popped it into her mouth while continuing to nurse.

Rytsar certainly knows how to spoil a girl, she thought, chuckling to herself.

After Hope had finished and Brie tucked her away safely in the fancy crib, she hit the remote and watched with wonder as the lights dimmed and the twinkling stars appeared.

Brie shut the door quietly and turned to see Titov standing there.

"I will watch over her," he assured Brie.

She bowed her head slightly. "Thank you, Titov."

"It is my pleasure, Mrs. Davis."

"You can call me Brie, if you like. You *are* family now."

He shook his head. "It makes me uncomfortable. I've never liked the cheese."

Brie's eyes widened and she had to cover her mouth

before she burst out laughing. Once again, Titov had surprised her with his unique sense of humor.

With a playful smirk, she told him, "I would hate to make you uncomfortable in any way, so you may continue to call me Mrs. Davis."

"Very well."

He walked over to the door and stood at attention. Although Brie felt it was entirely unnecessary, she sensed that it was important to Titov.

Heading off to Rytsar's bedroom, Brie found the black and gold bikini Sir had picked out for her to wear. She undressed and put it on, then brushed out her hair in front of the mirror. Looking at her reflection, Brie was amazed by how quickly the pounds of baby weight had disappeared due to her breastfeeding Hope.

Grasping her round breasts proudly, she smiled in the mirror. Another benefit had been these impressive breasts. Not Lea-sized, but damn big nonetheless. Not only were these beauties excellent milk producers, but they looked smoking hot, especially in the sexy bikini Sir had chosen for her.

Walking out with confidence, Brie joined the two men. She found them both lying out on the beach, soaking in the rays of the sun.

"Hope is asleep with Titov on guard," she announced.

"Good," Rytsar said, lifting his head to eye her flattering swimsuit. She could feel his obvious approval and blushed when he winked at her.

Sir patted the towel between them. "Come join us, babygirl."

Brie lay on it, smiling as she enjoyed the warmth of the California sun on her skin and listened to the soothing sound of the waves rolling in.

She turned her head slowly to the left to look at Rytsar, who was lying on his back, his eyes closed. Her gaze slowly traveled from his muscular chest down to his tight swimsuit, which effectively showed off his manly assets.

"I can feel your eyes on me, *radost moya*," Rytsar said with a smirk, his eyes still closed.

Brie giggled and turned her head to the right. Sir was lying on his stomach, his head resting against his folded arms. Unlike Rytsar, his eyes were open and he was staring straight at her. The ravenous look in his gaze made her pussy wet.

Biting her bottom lip, Brie turned her head to look up at the bright blue sky. Sir and Rytsar had something planned for her—she could feel it in her bones.

The two experienced Doms kept her constantly on her toes.

She loved being challenged by these two and wondered if today might include Rytsar's favorite tool, a bondage scene, or even a dual flogging by both Masters. She shivered in delight at the thought.

Of course, there was always the chance it might be something new she'd never experienced before. Sir and Rytsar were wickedly creative, and they consistently came up with fresh ways to please and test her.

Patience had never been Brie's strong suit, so she snuck a peek at both men. Sir's intense gaze was still on her, and now Rytsar's was, too.

"Téa."

Brie felt the butterflies start. Sir only used his pet name for her when they were about to scene together. "Yes, Master?"

"Rytsar needs refreshment."

"*Da*, I do," the Russian growled, licking his lips seductively.

Brie smiled. "What would you like, Rytsar?"

"Chilled vodka…and you."

"I'll have the same," Sir stated.

Brie stood up, her heart racing as she bowed to Sir. "If it pleases you, Master."

She left both men on the beach and walked back into Rytsar's home. Brie had a soft spot for his beach house. He had taken her to this place after he'd won her bid at the Submissive Training Center auction. At the time, she'd had no idea he spoke English and could understand every word she'd said.

The sexy Russian had wanted to play out the warrior fantasy she'd written in class. He had taken her simple fantasy and transformed it into a real-life experience.

Brie had lived out every emotion, as well as the physical aspects, of the fantasy she had written. Rytsar had left her breathless and totally captivated by the end of that evening. She'd never forgotten that night or the passion he had inspired in her at this beach house.

Brie thought back on it as she poured two generous shots of Rytsar's favorite vodka and put several pickles on a small glass plate for them. She picked up two glasses of vodka in one hand and the plate in the other, then turned to rejoin the Doms, but stopped short when she saw both men standing just outside the kitchen area.

"Kneel," Sir commanded.

She gracefully lowered herself to the marble floor as she'd been taught and then bowed her head in reverence.

Sir and Rytsar each took a shot glass and a pickle from her plate. Brie heard the clink of the glasses as the two men silently toasted each other, low chuckles filling the room.

Oh, these two were experts at teasing her! Not knowing what they were planning had Brie wet with anticipation.

"We are retiring to the bedroom, *radost moya*," Rytsar explained.

Sir then added his command. "Join us after you take a shot of vodka yourself, and undress."

Brie watched them leave and smiled to herself. Serving both Doms at the same time was a submissive's dream.

She dutifully poured herself a shot and threw it back before consuming a small, delightfully sour, dill pickle. The smooth vodka quickly warmed her insides, making her feel even friskier.

Taking off her bikini, she laid it on the counter before approaching Rytsar's closed bedroom door.

Brie was surprised to find the door shut and knocked softly. "Master?"

"You may enter, téa."

She unconsciously held her breath as she opened the door and walked inside. Letting out her breath slowly, Brie took in the sight of both men standing beside each other in all their naked glory.

Brie loved Sir's masculine body. He was tall, with a

head of dark hair and that sexy five o'clock shadow that outlined his chiseled jaw. Dark hair covered his toned chest and framed his impressive shaft, which happened to be the most handsome cock she'd ever seen.

Rytsar was Sir's perfect counterpart. Equally tall, he had no hair on his head. No, the Russian was sexy bald, with a strong jaw and riveting blue eyes. His broad chest and ripped abs complemented that majestic dragon tattoo on his left shoulder, which now bore her name.

"Do you remember the gift I purchased for you but we never had the chance to use, *radost moya*?" Rytsar asked.

Being that he was an extremely generous man, Brie was embarrassed to find herself at a loss. She looked to Sir for help, but he only smiled at her.

"I'm sorry, Rytsar," she admitted, blushing intensely. "I do not."

Both men stepped sideways, revealing the sex machine set on the floor behind them.

Brie squeaked in surprised delight, remembering the extravagant gift Rytsar had surprised her with when Sir had been in the hospital. It was known for giving women multiple orgasms because of the dual stimulation of its vibration and rotation. The machine itself looked similar to a leather saddle that a woman could "ride" and it was completely customizable.

For today's session, Rytsar had attached a large, chocolate brown phallus to the machine she would straddle. The cock was realistic looking and intimidating in its girth.

"You want me to ride that?"

"*Da*," Rytsar said with a wicked grin…

Cocky Russian

Although the size of the shaft on the machine had her feeling trembly and weak-kneed, she still very much wanted to try it.

"Come, téa," Sir said, holding his hand out to her.

Brie walked forward and grasped her Master's hand for support. She noticed that the cock had already been prepared for her and was liberally coated with lubricant. She gave a nervous giggle as she settled above it and slowly descended onto the huge head of the shaft.

Biting her lip, Brie forced her muscles to relax to encourage the invasion of the giant phallus.

"That's it," Rytsar growled huskily as the dark shaft slowly disappeared into her pussy.

Brie knelt on the floor, straddling the machine with the shaft deep inside her.

The position gave her the ability to grind against the cock as if it were real.

Rytsar held up a set of controls. "Now for the fun."

He turned on the power. The machine buzzed loudly, and Brie felt the vibration from her pussy all the way deep inside. She closed her eyes and began grinding against the toy, enjoying the unique stimulation it was creating.

That's when the Russian sadist turned the power up. Her eyes popped open as her entire body was rocked by the intense vibration.

"Oh, my God!"

Sir took the controls from Rytsar and stared at her lustfully as he turned the other dial. Brie's eyes widened as the cock began rotating in a circle—the huge shaft rubbing against her G-spot in slow, rhythmic motions.

Rytsar chuckled lustfully. "Now she understands the power behind the stallion."

Brie held her breath when her body suddenly tensed, readying for an orgasm. "Permission to come?" she begged, knowing she could not prevent it.

"That is the plan, téa," Sir answered smoothly. "Come for your Master."

Brie felt tremendous relief because the intensity of the machine-created climax was building with each rotation as her entire pussy shook from the vibration.

She closed her eyes and let the sensation take over…

Both men groaned when she threw her head back, screaming in passion as her body shuddered in the throes of a powerful orgasm.

Thankfully, Sir turned off the machine afterward, giving her sensitive clit time to recover.

She sat there looking up at both men, breathing hard and smiling like a kid. "That was freakin' amazing!"

"Good," Sir said, leaning down to cup her chin before kissing her. "We plan to make you come repeatedly with it."

Brie's heart skipped a beat. She knew from experience that multiple orgasms could prove just as challenging as orgasm denial.

However, she felt up for the challenge.

Rytsar positioned himself on her left and Sir on her right, their shafts hard and ready for her oral skills.

Sir turned the machine back on and commanded, "Open."

Brie grasped his cock and kept her eyes on him as she took his shaft into her mouth. Sir moved her hair to the side and held it there, so he could watch. She took his shaft as deeply as she could, then pulled back, trying again.

"That's it, téa…"

Brie swallowed, allowing the head of his shaft to travel slowly down her throat. She took him deeper and deeper until her lips touched the very base of his shaft. Once there, she began rocking gently back and forth, letting her throat caress his cock with its tight constriction.

The movement of her mouth, in unison with the rhythmic stimulation of her G-spot from the wicked cock inside her, caused an orgasm so intense that she had to stop deep-throating him when she came.

Brie grinned up at Sir afterward and apologized.

Rytsar, who was obviously turned on by watching her, demanded in a gruff voice, "I want that mouth."

Brie turned her head toward the Russian.

"Take him down your throat while you stroke my

cock," Sir ordered.

Brie sucked in several deep breaths before opening her mouth and taking Rytsar between her lips and relaxing her throat. Rytsar fisted her hair, guiding her movements while he slowly thrust his cock into her mouth.

Brie managed to keep stroking Sir's cock with her hand despite the added distraction of the machine's intense stimulation. Rytsar went excruciatingly slow as he forced his shaft down her throat. The Russian watched her hungrily as he let go of her hair and she pulled back to catch her breath.

She licked and nibbled the sides of his cock before encasing the head of his shaft again. Both men watched in rapt attention as her lips slowly moved from the head of his cock down to its base as she took his entire shaft down her throat.

Brie willingly became his vessel of pleasure when Rytsar roared in pleasure, fisting her hair again as he began fucking her mouth.

The fact was, the feel of his cock pumping in and out of her mouth complemented the movement of the cock rotating inside her, and she came again, moaning against his shaft as she climaxed.

He forced her to hold still, then commanded her to stop, playfully scolding her for almost taking him over the edge.

Brie loved hearing that she had brought Rytsar that close to losing control.

She turned her attention back on Sir, keeping her hand on Rytsar's cock so she could pleasure him while sucking her Master. The low, guttural sound of Sir's pleasure when she took him back into her mouth made Brie gush, covering the sexy machine with her excitement.

Sir pulled out, then pushed his cock slowly back into her mouth, running his fingers through her hair. "My good girl…"

Sir's praise had a physical effect on her because she instantly came again.

Rytsar smirked. "It seems *radost moya* enjoys the stallion. We could switch out the cock for a more challenging double penetration attachment, *moy droog.*"

Sir looked down at Brie with open desire and shook his head. "No, I prefer doing DP the old-fashioned way, old friend."

Brie nodded enthusiastically with Sir's cock still in her mouth.

"Agreed, comrade," Rytsar growled huskily. "But I need more sucking from those lips before we release her from the stallion."

"Then I shall play with her body, while *téa* pleases you."

Brie dutifully returned her attention to Rytsar.

Sir knelt beside her and whispered in her ear, "I enjoy watching you in action while I explore your body."

Brie closed her eyes, concentrating on her Master's touch as she pleasured Rytsar with her oral talents.

Sir caressed and tugged on her nipples, ordering in a seductive voice, "Grind on the machine."

Brie moaned around Rytsar's cock as she pressed her wet pussy against the vibrating machine, forcing the phallus even deeper inside her. Chills ran through Brie as her body tensed for another climax—but when this one hit, it didn't seem to end.

When Brie finally pulled back from Rytsar's cock to take a breath, Sir grabbed her breasts in both hands and descended on a nipple, sucking hard as she continued to grind against the machine.

She cried out in blissful pleasure, the multiple points of stimulation driving her absolutely crazy. "Oh, my God! I…can't…stop coming."

Both men chuckled, enjoying her heightened state of arousal.

"Look at me, *radost moya*," Rytsar commanded.

Brie gazed up at him with tears in her eyes—it felt so good.

"Do you like my cocky gift?"

She nodded, coming again as he asked.

Sir turned off the machine, but Brie's whole body continued to buzz from the ghosts of the vibration. He helped her disengage from it and Rytsar picked her weakened body up, carrying her to the bathroom to clean Brie in preparation for their next scene.

Brie was already flying high from her ride on the machine and squeaked when he touched her clit in the process of cleaning her.

"Are we sensitive?" he asked with a wicked grin.

Knowing he was a sadist, Brie was reluctant to tell him the truth but knew better than to deny it. "Yes, Rytsar."

He raised an eyebrow as he fingered her pussy. "Your pussy is burning hot, *radost moya*. I must fuck it now!" he declared, carrying her back into the bedroom where Sir was waiting for them on the oversized bed.

Rytsar set her down on it and joined her. He lay on his back and pulled her onto him. Brie straddled Rytsar like she had the machine. Rubbing her pussy over his cock, she could still feel the echoes of its vibration as she coated Rytsar's hard shaft with her excitement.

When he could take no more, the Russian guided his cock into her, grunting as he thrust. "Oh, you are fiery hot!" He grabbed the back of her head, kissing her forcefully on the lips as he thrust deeper into her.

Sir changed positions, moving behind Brie. "Your ass calls to your Master, téa."

Brie felt butterflies start when Sir began caressing her buttocks. Soon, the cold chill of lubricant followed as Sir slowly inserted his lubricated finger into her ass to help relax her inner muscles for the double penetration.

Brie then heard the slick, sexy sound of Sir lubricating his shaft. Wiping his hands, Sir tossed the hand towel to the floor and grabbed her hips. "Let me inside..."

Brie's pussy contracted with desire, squeezing Rytsar's shaft when Sir pressed the head of his cock against her taut opening. He slowly forced his rigid cock into her ass, causing her to cry out when he breached her opening and sank inside.

Sir threw his head back and groaned. "God, I love the feel of you."

Brie rocked against his cock, wanting this—needing to be penetrated by both men.

She whimpered when she felt Rytsar's teeth on her neck, giving her a sensual bite as Sir rolled his hips against her, forcing his cock deeper.

"Damn...she *is* extremely hot," Sir growled, reaching around to play with her nipples, helping her body to relax and take him even deeper. A tingling chill coursed through her body when she finally took the fullness of both their cocks, her body surrendering to it.

Rytsar sought out her lips as he and Sir claimed her.

Brie's pussy could not resist the pressure of dual cocks moving inside her, and she soon felt the telltale signs of an intense climax building.

"I'm about to come again," she whispered.

Rytsar let out a low growl. "I'm going to pump my seed deep into your pussy when you do."

Brie whimpered, her orgasm building to dangerous levels.

Sir responded by smacking her on the ass. The sexy sound of it echoed throughout the room, turning her on even more.

Rytsar groaned as he thrust his hips upward, forcing his cock all the way into her pussy as he gripped her ass. "Are you ready to be thoroughly fucked?"

Brie bit her lip and nodded.

The Russian pulled her down so that her torso lay on his chest while Sir repositioned himself behind her for deeper penetration. Brie screamed the first time they each gave her a full stroke in tandem. It was almost too much, but Sir commanded huskily, "Give in to it, téa."

Sir ramped things up, coordinating his thrusts with Rytsar's, as they released their passion on her body. Soft mews escaped Brie's lips as the exquisite sensations they were generating took control of her body—each thrust bringing her a symphony of pleasure.

Rytsar growled hoarsely, "Come for my cock, *radost moya*."

With her pussy stretched unnaturally tight by the two men, the pulsing sensation when her orgasm took hold was far more intense—and the rush of it heightened her senses.

Both men cried out as they followed her orgasm with their own, pumping her hard as they each came.

Pure submissive bliss…

Sir pulled out first and lay beside her while Brie continued to rest her cheek on Rytsar's chest, listening to his heart beat rapidly. She was enjoying the stillness, floating in the unique subspace their dual penetration had evoked.

Sir's lusty groan, coupled with a slap on the ass, caused her pussy to start pulsing and she milked Rytsar's spent shaft with one last orgasm. Afterward, Sir pulled her to him and kissed her.

Wrapping his arms around Brie, he nuzzled her neck, holding her captive in his embrace. "I love you."

Her heart fluttered whenever he said those three words.

"This Russian loves you, too, *radost moya*," Rytsar stated, gazing at her with those intense blue eyes. "And I am about to show you how much…"

He got up from the bed and Brie watched as Rytsar opened his toy chest and went through it. He meticulously laid out each item one by one in a neat row on his dresser—a set of nipple clamps, a pair of cuffs, a bejeweled butt plug, a spreader bar, and his wicked cat o' nines.

Brie stared at the array of tools, her heart beating faster.

Sir leaned over and nibbled her ear. "Téa, are you ready for our next round?"

Oh, yes…please.

Brie headed back to Rytsar's bedroom after finishing Hope's early morning five o'clock feeding, wanting to sleep a few more hours. She was thoroughly exhausted after yesterday's energetic play session.

She noticed Rytsar was missing from the bed when she entered the bedroom, but the bathroom door was slightly ajar.

Naturally curious after spotting a glimpse of him, she walked closer to peek through the doorway.

Rytsar stood at the sink with a towel wrapped around his waist as he shaved his head. He was so focused on the task that he didn't notice her standing there.

His movements were slow and meticulous as he dragged the razor over his scalp and cleaned off the blade before making another pass.

The entire time, he stared intently into the mirror as if he were seeing someone. Brie imagined it must be Tatianna, and tears came to her eyes.

She suddenly understood that ever since Tatianna's death, Rytsar started each day like this, shaving his head in mourning of her.

The thought of that caused a painful lump in her throat.

His love for Tatianna continued to burn bright despite all the years that had passed since her death.

After Rytsar finished, he wiped his clean-shaven head with a hand towel, then stared at the mirror for a moment before leaning forward to whisper something.

A tear ran down Brie's cheek.

She was certain he was speaking to Tatianna. How beautifully tragic that he re-connected with her every morning and that she remained a part of his life.

Rytsar was a condor, like Sir.

He turned to walk out, stopping short when he saw her. "*Radost moya*, what are you doing here?"

Instead of answering him, Brie walked up to him, wrapping her arms around his muscular body as she laid her head on his chest. "You are a beautiful soul."

His low chuckle reverberated against her cheek as he enfolded her in his strong embrace.

Laugh with Lea

With their big move-in date quickly approaching, Brie was tickled when Lea offered to come over and help her pack some of her personal things.

"I can just imagine it. A day of constant giggling," Sir stated when she told him.

Brie had to laugh because she knew he was right. "We'll do our best to keep it to a minimum, Sir."

"No need." He cupped her chin and kissed her on the lips. "I enjoy the sound of your happiness." Her heart melted as he pulled away.

"I'll keep Hope with us so you don't have to worry about her while you work, Sir," she assured him.

"Actually, I plan to take time off to spend the day with her."

Brie's hands flew to her chest as she cooed. "Oh my goodness...a daddy/daughter day! How sweet is that?"

He smiled tenderly as he looked at Hope, who was happily bouncing in her jumper.

Brie remembered Sir's promise that he would be an

active parent in Hope's life, just as his father had been in his. And, despite his heavy workload, Sir had kept that vow, changing diapers without complaint, comforting Hope in the night, and even joining Brie for pediatrician check-ups.

He was nothing like Brie's own father, who had pretty much come home every night after work expecting his wife to wait on him hand and foot.

Her mother had done so happily, never questioning his lack of involvement in Brie's life. In their household, clear lines had been drawn between the male and female roles and were strictly adhered to.

Seeing the interaction between Sir and Hope made Brie wonder what her relationship with her father would have been like if he'd been equally involved when she was a child.

Knowing there was no point in dwelling on what might have been, Brie dismissed the thought. However, it did make her even more grateful for the role Sir had chosen to take in their own little family.

People on the outside naturally assumed that because they had a D/s relationship, that those same old-fashioned rules applied. But, nothing could be further from the truth.

Sir cherished her and his child, and, because of that, he would do anything to keep them safe and well cared for, both physically and emotionally.

While the dynamics of their power exchange were polar opposites, the two of them were still equal partners—both having a voice in what happened in and out of the bedroom. Brie knew that Sir valued her thoughts and opinions, and he considered them with every decision he made.

Brie credited their commitment to the BDSM lifestyle for ensuring they practiced open communication in all other aspects of their lives.

It was perfectly acceptable for her to disagree with Sir but, in those rare instances when she did, he encouraged her to respectfully voice her reasoning so they could discuss it and come to a mutual understanding.

Oftentimes, once he explained his decision-making process, she agreed with him. The few times when they could not come to an agreement, Brie acquiesced, trusting in his dominance over her. However, there had been several times when Sir had taken her side because, although he did not agree, he could see it was important to her.

Brie was grateful that Sir took his dominant position in her life seriously, and that he never made her feel less important because she served under him as his submissive.

She figured her father could learn a thing or two about being a real man from Sir.

Wouldn't that be an interesting discussion? She thought, giggling to herself.

Brie stood by the door, eagerly awaiting Lea's arrival. As soon as Brie heard the ding of the elevator, she swung it open and cried, "Lea!"

Lea's face lit up and she ran to Brie, hugging her in the hallway. "I can never get enough of my Stinky Cheese."

"And this Funky Fromage can't get enough of you," Brie answered.

Pulling her into the apartment, Brie started giggling like a schoolgirl.

"I remember this," Sir said with a smirk.

"Hello, Sir Davis," Lea said, bowing in respect. "I'm really looking forward to seeing your new place."

He glanced at Brie and gave her a wink. "So is my wife."

Lifting Hope up, he told them, "I'll leave you ladies to it while Hope and I spend time learning about quantum physics."

Sir headed down the hallway, whistling a catchy tune. Brie remembered it from hearing recordings of his father playing the violin. It touched her that Sir made sure that Alonzo was a part of Hope's life. He kissed Hope on the top of her head before entering the bedroom and shutting the door behind him.

"Was he serious?" Lea asked, laughing.

Brie smiled. "He is, actually. It's the sweetest thing, too."

Lea gave her a look of disbelief. "I don't believe you for a second."

"I'm completely serious, woman. Instead of reading children's books to Hope, Sir reads whatever book he's currently into."

"And he's reading quantum physics for fun?"

Brie shrugged. "He likes to keep up on the latest

stuff. It's stimulating for him."

Lea shook her head, laughing. "If I didn't respect Sir Davis so much, I'd make a joke about him right now."

"It's probably wise that you don't," Brie said, elbowing her.

"So, how does Hope handle that kind of reading material?"

"She eats it up. That little girl loves listening to her daddy. She just stares at him as he talks." Brie got out her phone and showed Lea a video she had taken of Sir reading to the baby. The expression on Hope's face as she looked up at him was one of pure adoration and wonder.

"Aww…" Lea squeaked. "That is too stinkin' cute."

"I know," Brie said, looking at her phone tenderly. "I could watch those two together all day long."

Lea took the phone from her and laid it on the counter. "But we aren't going to do that, because I came here to work. So, tell me what you want me to do."

"Let's finish up the baby's room."

"Sounds like a plan, Stan." Lea marched down the hallway, but instead of turning into Hope's room, she continued down the hallway and pressed her ear against the door to their bedroom.

"Lea…" Brie whispered.

Lea turned her head and put her finger to her lips before pressing her head against the door again. She put her hand to her heart as she listened, an enchanted look on her face.

Finally, she moved away from the door and walked back to Brie. "Oh, my! If I could just bottle up that man's voice, I could make millions. Even I was trans-fixed, and I don't know a damn thing about quantum physics."

"I wouldn't be surprised if she does. Of course, hearing him read *Goodnight Moon* would put him off the charts on the cuteness scale."

Brie smiled. "I have to admit that seeing a man being a good daddy does something to my ovaries."

"Yeah, like seeing a sexy man holding a puppy."

Laughing, Brie told her, "I'm partial to babies…but, yeah."

Lea walked into the guestroom and frowned. "It looks like you've already done most of the packing."

"Nope, there's still the closet, and trust me, I have a lot of my old stuff I have to finish sifting through. Thankfully, it's going to be tons more fun with you here."

"That's exactly why I came!" she said, opening up the closet door and grabbing a tote. "I make the world a more fun place."

"Yes, you do," Brie agreed wholeheartedly, giving her a hug.

Lea squeezed her back before ripping off the lid of a tote.

"Oh…!" Brie cried in delight.

"What?" Lea asked, peeking inside.

"This is the old video camera my parents got me when I was a kid." Brie held it up, a flood of memories washing over her as she stared at it.

Lea took it from her, handling it as if it were made of glass. "This…this belongs in a museum. The Brie

Bennett-Davis Director Museum."

"Yeah, right," Brie said, trying to take it back.

Lea moved it out of her reach. "No, I'm serious, girl-friend. You're going to be famous, and this will become a treasured item that fans everywhere will flock to see."

Brie burst out laughing. "I doubt that very much."

Lea held up the video camera, looking at it with reverence. "And this is the hallowed instrument that began her career in film."

Shaking her head, Brie took it from her and set it to the side. "So, this goes in the keeper pile."

Lea suddenly let out a squeal. "Are these all the films you made?"

Brie looked fondly at the mix of mini-cassette tapes. "Yep. It's like a digital diary of my life as a kid in Nebraska."

"Ooh...can I watch one?"

She shook her head, saying, "My life was extremely boring back then. Trust me. I'm sparing you by saying no. You really don't want to watch them."

"But I do..." she said, giving Brie puppy eyes. "I *really* do."

Brie giggled. "Fine. Someday we'll have a My Boring Life in Nebraska Party. But, today, we have to get all this sorted and packed."

"You promise, Stinky Cheese?"

Brie wrapped an arm around Lea, touched that she cared. "Yes, I promise."

Lea grabbed a roll of bubble wrap and started wrapping one of the tapes.

"What are you doing? They don't need to be

wrapped. Just throw them over here with the camera."

"Are you kidding? These are precious, Brie. You can't chance them being compromised because of the move."

Brie shook her head again. "Lea, you're freaking adorable."

"I don't want any of your devoted fans to say that I failed to protect these jewels."

She laughed. "Girl, when you watch them, you'll have another name for them, and it will start with S-H—"

Lea hugged the tape against her chest. "Don't you dare call them that."

The fact that Lea was being so protective of her first attempts at filmmaking was totally endearing to Brie. "I wish I could keep you in my pocket."

Lea giggled, putting the tape down for a moment in order to grab her huge breasts. "I'm not fitting in your pocket with these babies." She proudly looked down at her huge boobs. "Did you know they're a ton of fun to play with?"

Brie rolled her eyes. "No, I wouldn't know…"

Lea reached over and snatched her hand, placing it on her left breast. "Go ahead. I don't mind."

Brie looked at her hand, dwarfed by Lea's large breast, and did the first thing that came to mind. Squeezing it, she said, "Honk!" and burst out in snorting laughter.

"That's the best you can do?" Lea teased. "It's okay, Stinky Cheese. If I had little boobies like yours, I wouldn't know what to do with these babies, either."

Brie looked down at her own breasts. "Girl, there is

nothing little about my melons. Breastfeeding Hope has made them huge."

Bouncing her boobs up and down with her hands, Lea said proudly, "But nothing can compare to mine."

"True," Brie giggled. "You *are* the biggest boob I know."

Lea elbowed her with a twinkle in her eye. "You're getting there, honey. Don't worry. Someday, you'll almost be as funny as me."

After she finished wrapping and taping the cassette tape thoughtfully, she stared at it. "You know, Brie…"

She assumed Lea was going to say something about her films. "Yes?"

"I've got a joke for you."

"Oh, lord…" Brie groaned with amusement.

"How many directors does it take to screw in a light bulb?"

Brie grinned. "I don't know, Lea. How many directors does it take to screw in a light bulb?"

"Directors don't screw in a light bulb, silly. They screw in a hot tub."

Even though the joke was bad, Brie couldn't stop laughing.

Lea just nodded in proud satisfaction. "After all these years, I've still got it."

Brie shook her head as she pulled out another tote.

"So, Lea, Sir asked me to make a decision about which film to work on next. What do you think? Should I finish the second documentary or jump into the documentary about Alonzo Davis and his magical violin?"

Lea stopped wrapping the tape she was holding and looked up at Brie. "Naturally, I'd love to see my scene with Tono on the big screen, but you have to follow your heart, girlfriend."

Her answer caused Brie to think back on all those incredible scenes she'd filmed for the follow-up documentary.

It would be a shame if the world didn't get a chance to see the talent of Tono and his unique version of Kinbaku, Master Anderson's hot bullwhip session with Boa or the incredible skills of Marquis Gray.

Damn… there were so many worthy scenes.

The moments she'd captured on film were like her babies and, if Brie did nothing, they would never see the light of day.

However, she did not relish the idea of working with Mr. Holloway again, and there was no way that she would allow him to delete the scene with Marquis Gray. This was *her* film, and she trusted her instincts. "I really don't like Holloway, Lea, but I'm thinking it might be worth the fight if he can help get this second film out. At the very least, I'll get a better handle on what's happening with Mary. She's been so closed-mouthed about what's going on between them."

"It can't be good. I have been worried about that girl…" Lea stated. "Mary may be a bitch, but she's our fucking bitch."

Brie smiled, her heart full of compassion for Mary. "She's been there for both of us when we needed her."

Lea nodded, frowning slightly. "Yeah, if I had just listened to her…"

"Nope, we're not going there." Brie knew that Lea still blamed herself for not listening to Mary's warning about Liam. Because of that, something terrible almost happened. Lea still held herself responsible for the attempted kidnapping of Brie and Hope.

"Liam was *not* your fault. None of the bad things that happened had anything to do with you." Brie stopped what she was doing. She felt it was important to enforce her words with a hug.

"How is your heart, my friend?" she whispered as she squeezed Lea, knowing that she struggled with having loved Liam before it all went crashing down in flames.

Lea let out a long sigh. "My heart is slowly healing."

"Is there anything I can do to make it heal faster?"

"Yes, there is."

Brie broke away to look her in the eye. "Name it, girlfriend."

"Tell me a joke."

"Lea..." she complained. "I'm being serious here."

"I'm being serious, too. You don't know the power a good joke has for me, Brie. And, for it to come from my best friend? I would love nothing more. Seriously."

Brie wondered if Lea was teasing her, but the desperate look in her eyes spurred Brie on to try. "Let's see..." She laughed uncomfortably after a moment. "I didn't realize how hard this would be. Coming up with a joke bad enough to be Lea-worthy is not an easy task."

"I believe in you, girl," Lea encouraged her, giving two thumbs up.

Brie sifted through all the bad jokes she knew, trying

to find one that Lea hadn't already told her. "I think I have a good one."

"Great!" Lea clapped her hands excitedly.

"It's a clown joke."

"Even better. I love clowns."

"I have no idea why when they creep me out." Brie shuddered. "But this one is totally you."

"Hit me with it, sister."

"What do you call a clown who gives his girlfriend flowers?"

Before Lea had time to think, Brie blurted out the punch line. "A romantic jester!"

"Aww…that's so cute, Brie."

"But it didn't make you laugh," she said sadly.

Lea patted her on the back. "It takes years of practice to be as talented as I am."

Brie was disappointed. "I'm sorry it didn't help, Lea."

Lea answered her apology with a hug. "But it did help. You made a bad joke just for me. That's what true friendship is all about."

"Seriously, if you need anything, just let me know. I'm here for you one hundred percent, girlfriend."

Lea's smile was genuine when she told Brie, "I know, it means so much to me that you have my back."

"Forever and always."

"Same here." After another squishy hug with those big boobs, she said, "Do you know what the title associate director really means?"

Brie felt another joke coming on and answered hesitantly, "No, what does the title associate director really mean?"

"He's the only guy in Hollywood who will associate with the director." Lea giggled, adding, "No matter what kind of fallout happens in life, Stinky Cheese, I'll always be your associate director."

Moving Day

A fter three weeks of renovations, Sir finally made the announcement Brie had been patiently waiting for. "The house is ready and I've hired a moving crew to finish the packing and transport everything tomorrow."

"Oh, my goodness, that's fast!" Brie couldn't believe they would be leaving their apartment in the morning and living in their new home that same night.

"The sooner we start this next chapter in our lives, the better. Don't you agree?"

She nodded, her heart beating fast at the thought. "If we're moving in tomorrow, does that mean I can ask what the big surprise is now? I've been dying to know, but have been your patient girl."

He smiled at her tenderly. "Yes, you have."

"So, you'll tell me?"

"Actually, I prefer that you discover it for yourself."

"Oh, like an Easter egg hunt?" She was thrilled by the idea. "Will I be looking for something big or small?"

Sir raised an eyebrow, letting her know he wasn't giving her any hints.

Brie suddenly realized how devious he was. Their simple exchange had her anticipating the hunt, which was going to make the wait that much harder on her. "I see what you did there, Sir."

He winked at her. "It's my duty and honor to challenge you."

Brie pouted in protest, making Sir laugh.

"Aren't you going to thank me for being such a thoughtful Master, babygirl?"

"Thank you, Master. Truly, your thoughtfulness knows no bounds," she joked.

Tweaking her nose, he told her, "When you see it, you'll know it was worth the wait."

"I'm sure I will, Sir."

Every word he said was just making it harder on her, and he knew it.

Such a cruel Master...

Even though she had protested the wait, Brie was glad Sir was challenging her in her areas of weakness—especially when that challenge included a special surprise.

Wrapping her arms around his waist, Brie purred. "Despite the cruelty of your ways, dear Master, this sub loves you."

Sir put his finger under her chin and lifted it to meet his gaze. "Despite your lack of patience, little sub, this Master loves you, too."

Brie stood on tiptoes to kiss his sexy chin. "Do you really think you'll ever be able to teach me patience?"

He smirked. "With a lifetime ahead of us, I'm certain I will."

Eep!

By eight the next morning, the house was flooded by a large crew of movers, one for every room in the apartment.

Sir had already managed to get Shadow into a cat carrier without suffering any damage.

"How the heck did you do that?" Brie asked, genuinely impressed.

"I'll never tell."

"But you *are* planning to mention that you accomplished this magical feat to Rytsar, aren't you?"

He smirked. "It's possible."

Brie giggled, knowing Rytsar would be impressed after the amount of damage he suffered doing the same thing.

Watching the workers moving about efficiently, she told him, "I didn't expect there would be so many."

"The sooner they pack and move our things, the sooner we can relax in our new home."

"New home…" Tears came to Brie's eyes. "It almost seems too good to be true, Sir." She walked over to the expansive window and looked down at the city below. "But, I will miss this place."

Sir walked up behind her and stated. "I will miss aspects of this apartment, as well."

She turned to face him and smiled. "I'll never forget when you brought me up here the first time. I was a bundle of nerves."

"I was anxious myself, having just quit my headmaster position."

She looked up into his eyes. "I still can't believe you did that for me."

Sir kissed her gently on the lips. "Best spontaneous decision I ever made, Mrs. Davis."

One of the movers came up, asking, "Mister, would you like us to wrap this lounge chair in plastic wrap or moving blankets?"

Sir gave Brie a private smile before telling the man, "I don't want the leather of this fine chair damaged. Make it both."

"Very well, sir."

Brie stared at the red tantra chair and murmured softly so only Sir could hear, "I remember the first time I sat down in that chair, having no clue what it was..."

"Oh, I remember that quite well," Sir replied in a low, husky voice that made her body quiver.

So many sexy memories were attached to that chair, and the man beside her was part of every single one of them.

"Miss, pardon me, but how would you like the kitchen items separated?" a woman asked.

Brie smiled at Sir. He still did most of the cooking, but she told him, "I'll handle this." Giving him a respectful nod, Brie headed into the kitchen to direct her.

In a matter of a few short hours, the crew had the entire place packed and were beginning the task of carting everything out to the elevator for the long ride down to the moving van outside.

"We're no longer needed here, and hauling this will take some time. Fortunately, Marquis Gray and Celestia have offered to watch Hope and Shadow for us while we get all the furniture situated and essentials unpacked in the new house."

"That's sweet of them."

"They're good people," he stated.

Brie took Sir's hand and squeezed it. "They certainly are. You're surrounded by a bunch of good friends."

Sir chuckled lightly. "I would never have believed it when I first started college. If I knew then what the future held, I might not have been such a recluse when I started out."

"I love that the friends you made then still remain your friends now."

Sir held out his arm to her. "Thankfully, my circle of friends has grown considerably since then."

As he led Brie to the door, she glanced back, saying wistfully, "I'm going to really miss this place."

"No reason to miss it yet, my dear. We'll be coming back later."

Brie was relieved. She needed some private time to say goodbye to the apartment that held so many special memories.

Sir rushed to drop Hope and Shadow off, wanting to get to the house before the movers arrived.

"I've been looking forward to seeing your face when you see my surprise."

With less than an hour's drive to their new house, Sir had managed, yet again, to take her impatience up a notch.

"Cruel, cruel Master…"

He stared at the road ahead, smiling to himself.

Brie figured it had to be something spectacular for Sir to be acting like this, and it made the waiting that much harder when they were stopped in a traffic jam on the highway.

Determined to show Sir an outward appearance of calm, Brie stared straight ahead with a blissful smile on her lips.

When he *finally* pulled up to the house, she let out an audible sigh of relief.

"Anxious to run in there?" Sir asked.

"A patient sub wouldn't run," she answered.

Sir seemed to purposely take his time getting out of the car before walking over to open the door for her. She took a deep breath, keeping her blissful demeanor intact as she took his hand and got out.

But all pretense disappeared when she stood there, looking at their new house, and was suddenly overcome with emotion.

Our children will grow up in this house…

Sir told her to wait while he walked up and unlocked the door. Coming back for her, he swept her up into his arms and carried her through the doorway. "Welcome home, Brie."

He set her down, his eyes sparkling with excitement.

It suddenly dawned on her that Sir was every bit as excited as she was, and knowing that gave her butterflies.

After Sir shut the door, he said, "Before you go searching for my gift, I'd like you to take a look at the kitchen."

Brie had wanted to see the new counters they had picked out together and rushed over to see them. "Oh,

Sir…it looks even better than I imagined," she cooed, running her hands over the black marble countertops with streaks of white crystals running throughout. "It's so elegant."

"I agree. I think we did well in choosing this."

"We will feed our army in elegance."

"Among other things," he added in a seductive voice. "You will look absolutely delectable splayed out on this counter.

Goosebumps rose on Brie's skin, imagining laying on the cold counter with Sir staring hungrily at her.

Sir leaned down to kiss her lightly on the lips. "Your lesson in patience is over, téa."

His words made her giddy. Not only was he giving her permission to run like a little kid through the house, but he had called her by her pet name, which meant a scene was in her near future.

"Thank you, Master!"

Brie let out a happy squeak as she made a beeline to the bedroom first, expecting to see some kind of fantasy suite. When she swung the doors open, she saw that it was just as it was before—an empty room with an incredible view of the ocean, except…

Sir had added a reading nook in the corner with built-in bookshelves.

"That's lovely, Sir," she said, trying desperately not to sound disappointed.

He smiled at her knowingly. "That's not the surprise."

Brie grinned, unable to hide her relief. "There's more?"

When he nodded, she resumed her hunt. Knowing the bathroom was already a dream come true, Brie headed upstairs, taking two stairs at a time. When she arrived at the top, she saw an elegant desk in the loft, facing the view of the ocean.

"Oh, Sir, is this for me?" she asked in wonderment.

"I had this desk custom built. I want you to have only the best for your office."

She wrapped her arms around him, touched that he cared so much about supporting her career. "I love it, Sir. This is absolutely beautiful, and the fact that you had the desk made for me makes it even more special."

Sir took her hand and kissed it. "I consider it an honor to support your career, my love."

The butterflies started up again and she wondered if the time had come to christen the kitchen countertops.

Instead, Sir whispered into her ear, "This isn't it either."

"More?" she squeaked, unable to contain her excitement.

When Sir nodded, Brie checked all the rooms upstairs before heading back down to the first level.

She became methodical as she checked the dining room, the formal office, and the guest bedroom, but she came up short.

Remembering the hot tub outside, she headed out to check, certain she'd finally discovered his surprise.

Although some of the vines on the lattice had started to bloom with purple flowers, nothing had changed.

Brie was stumped and looked at Sir questioningly. Maybe it *was* the bathroom? It was possible Sir hadn't liked the theme and had altered it.

Heading back into the master bedroom, she walked straight to the bathroom to find it was the same lovely bathroom, with the Roman columns and Italian tile.

Brie was thoroughly stumped.

Afraid she had missed some small detail, she walked through the entire house again. After combing through every room, she was at a complete loss.

Putting her hands on her hips, she frowned in defeat. "Other than the counters, the reading nook, and the desk upstairs, I don't see a difference, Sir."

"You haven't looked closely enough," Sir stated with amusement.

Brie let out a frustrated sigh. "I checked the whole house, so unless there's a hidden room I don't know about…"

She saw that sparkle return to his eyes and knew she was on to something. She returned to the bedroom and opened the walk-in closet only to find it was unchanged.

She then headed for the giant shoe closet on the other side of the bedroom, and that's when it hit her. The door to the shoe closet was gone as if it had never existed.

Next to where it was supposed to be was the new bookcase, as well as the newly built window seat. She'd been so intent on finding the obvious that she had totally missed what was no longer there.

Pointing to the missing closet door, she asked excitedly, "What happened to the shoe closet, Sir?"

Smiling, Sir called out, "Open the door. Five-two-one-one-four."

Brie heard a click and the wall slowly swung open. She walked over to it completely enchanted by having a secret room.

When she stepped inside, Brie put her hand to her mouth. "Oh, my goodness, Sir."

The room had been completely gutted of all the shoe shelves. Instead, it had been transformed into their own private playroom.

The crimson walls had iron hooks and shelving to store their multitude of toys, along with a St. Andrew's Cross, a spanking bench, inviting chains hanging from above, and the most exciting thing of all…a wooden table with leather cuffs attached to it.

Brie swore it looked like the table at the Submissive Training Center. The same table that Sir had bound her to on her second day of training and then had taken her virginal ass for the first time.

"Is that…?" she asked breathlessly.

"No, it's a replica I had made."

Brie shook her head as she walked up to it, the memories of their first time flooding through her mind. "This table was the beginning of us."

"Yes. In a sense, it was," he agreed.

Looking around the room, she said, "I can't believe you created this."

"I took Gallant's example, wanting to preserve our relationship by keeping it out of sight." He glanced at the table. "As far as that, I could think of no other furniture you would enjoy more. You've always been partial to the bondage table."

"It was the first thing that caught my attention on

the website. I remember how much I wanted to be that girl bound on the table in that picture..."

Brie closed her eyes, reveling in the feelings of love and excitement stirring inside. "This is perfect Sir."

"I'm glad you approve, téa," he said, kissing her deeply.

Brie always loved hearing him call her by that name and assumed the scene had begun. "How would you like me, Master?"

"While I would love to bind you to this table and make you scream my name as I fuck you, we will have to wait. The movers will be arriving soon."

Brie wanted to protest but she knew he was right. Leaving the room with him, she watched as Sir shut the door by calling out, "Close. Five-two-one-one-four."

The lock slid into place, and it became a seamless wall again.

"You will need to use the number to unlock it. Can you remember it?" he asked.

Brie thought for a second before saying the numbers, five-two-one-four-one."

"Close." He repeated the correct number.

After Brie said it correctly, he told her, "We will program it to recognize your voice, so only you and I will be able to control it."

"That's amazing, Sir." Curious about the sequence of numbers, she asked, "Does that number have any significance?"

He smiled. "Yes, it's the day I knew my life would never be the same."

After doing some quick math in her head, Brie realized it was not only the day of her second session at the Training Center but the night Sir had taken her virginal ass. Her heart melted when she realized that encounter was as memorable to him as it was to her.

She gave him a grateful kiss. "It's the perfect number combination for our secret room."

"I agree, téa."

She felt a surge of sexual electricity on hearing him use her pet name again. It had her anticipating what he was planning, and she purred in excitement.

It was then that she heard the roar of the moving truck pulling up.

"Are you ready for a day of unpacking, my dear?"

Taking his hand in hers, she answered with an enthusiastic, "It would be my pleasure, Master."

Sir walked with her to the door, squeezing her hand. "After we are done here, I will claim what's mine."

She burned with desire on hearing his declaration, and spent the entire day unpacking in an elevated state of arousal.

Sexy Goodbyes

The head of the moving crew went over the paper-work with Sir to ensure that no box had been left behind. When everything had been accounted for, he held out his hand to Sir. "We're done here, Mr. Davis. Enjoy your new home."

Sir shook his hand firmly and handed over a gener-ous amount of cash. "This is for you and your crew. You did exceptional work here today. Thank you."

The man looked down at the large stack of bills and grinned. "Thank you, Mr. Davis!"

Nodding at Brie, the man left.

Once she heard the moving van pull away, Brie turned to Sir. Holding her breath in anticipation, she slowly lowered herself to the floor and bowed low at his feet.

"How may I serve you, Master?"

Her whole body quivered as she imagined all the things he would do to her.

Instead of giving her a command, however, he asked

for her hand and helped her back to her feet.

"Not here, téa," he said with a seductive smile. "Come with me."

Her heart skipped a beat as he placed his hand on the small of her back and she felt that familiar jolt of electricity that Sir's touch always caused.

Leading her out of the house, he took her to the car and drove her back to the apartment just as the sun was setting.

Downtown LA became a magical place as the colorful sunset brought out another side of the city, bathing the tall skyscrapers in fiery shades of orange and yellow.

That sense of magic continued as Brie walked into the building with Sir.

"Good evening, Mr. and Mrs. Davis."

Sir nodded to the doorman in acknowledgement while Brie kept her attention solely on Sir as he guided her to the elevator.

Déjà vu washed over her as all those memories of her first time here, when Sir brought her home after the collaring ceremony, came flooding back.

She'd been so nervous back then…

As they stood there, waiting for the elevator, Brie reconnected with those old feelings and unknowingly let out a nervous sigh.

"Nothing to be nervous about, babygirl."

She looked at him and smiled. He'd said that on the first night, too. She was curious if he was planning to replay that first night here, and she felt a thrill at the thought.

The bell chimed just before the elevator doors

opened. On the ride up, Brie stared discreetly at Sir in the reflection of the mirrored walls of the elevator.

Sir's chiseled good looks had matured over the last few years, giving him an even more commanding demeanor. She searched his face, trying to figure out the difference. He was just as handsome, but his look was leaner...and wiser.

Although Brie would never dare tell him that! She'd learned her lesson about using the word "wise" around Sir.

When they arrived on the fifteenth floor, Brie hesitated for a moment before stepping out.

This would be the last time...

Knowing that filled her with sadness. She had so many memories associated with this apartment.

Her entire life changed here!

Sir pressed his hand against her back, directing her forward as he escorted her to the dark wooden door of his apartment, which was engraved with the BDSM triskele. Brie wondered if the next tenant would understand the significance of the symbol.

When Sir opened the door, she entered the apartment hesitantly. She noticed her heels now made a hollow echo as she walked down the long, narrow hallway that was now bare of all the art that used to cover the walls.

Thankfully, for Brie, the apartment still smelled of Sir and made her smile.

They walked into the large, empty room with the floor-to-ceiling windows that overlooked downtown LA.

"I will miss this view," she murmured as the two of

them watched the last rays of the sun disappear behind the buildings.

Sir moved behind her, stating in a low growl, "It is an impressive view, but I know of one even better."

He slowly began undressing her, running his hands over her bare skin, as he removed each piece of clothing. Sir's light touch sent shivers through her, causing her nipples to ache with desire.

When she was completely naked except for his collar, Sir leaned down and murmured seductively as his lips grazed her neck, "I prefer you like this."

Brie let out a soft moan, loving the feel of his sensual lips on her skin.

"Walk to the window," he commanded.

Brie's heart raced, certain now that Sir was reenacting the first night when she came home with him.

"Spread your legs shoulder width apart, put your hands on the window, and lean forward so your nipples touch the glass."

Goosebumps rose on her skin as she opened her legs and put her palms against the window, leaning forward until her nipples touched the cold glass. There was a sense of vulnerability in being naked in front of the huge window with the city bustling below them. But that feeling was something she had come to enjoy.

Brie let out a soft gasp, reacting to the chilly temperature.

She distinctly remembered their first scene as Master and submissive, and she waited patiently as she stared at his reflection in the glass.

Sir stood back to admire her.

This was something that Brie had not only gotten used to but had come to crave—his lustful scrutiny of her body.

Sir stared at her for quite some time. She wondered if he was noting every detail so he wouldn't forget it, or if he was being flooded with old memories as she was.

As if in confirmation, he stated, "Know that I will think of you as a goddess even as I fuck you like a slut."

Her eyes widened, remembering those words that first night. They still had power over her, making her wet with desire.

Brie relished the unique stimulation of having her nipples pressed against the glass. The cool temperature made her nipples ache and she longed to feel his warm lips encasing them.

Sir moved up behind her and commanded in a deep voice. "Don't move or speak, but you are allowed to come."

His simple command made her pussy drip with excitement, knowing what was about to happen next.

He lightly traced his fingertips over her shoulders, causing her whole body to focus solely on his touch. She continued to sneak peeks at his reflection as he slowly lowered himself and began exploring her swollen pussy with his fingers.

Hearing his passionate grunt sent chills through her.

"Your body tells me everything I want to know, téa."

Brie struggled to keep silent as he began fingering her pussy. With such skilled fingers, Sir was quickly able to bring her to the edge.

Closing her eyes, she relaxed and gave in to the orgasm.

"Good girl," he murmured just before she felt his warm tongue on her throbbing clit.

Brie opened her eyes and suddenly let out a muffled squeak when she saw the silhouette of a woman standing at the window of the high rise across from them. She had her elbows up beside her head as if she were looking through a set of binoculars.

"I said not to make a sound," Sir chided, spanking her ass firmly.

Brie was unsure if this was part of Sir's plan or if the woman was an unwanted observer, so she broke her silence. "Sir…"

He grasped her ass cheeks with both hands. "This better be good."

Pointing, she told him, "There's someone watching us in the other building."

Sir stood up and looked in the direction she was indicating, obviously surprised to hear it.

"Ah…" he muttered in a thoughtful tone. After a moment of contemplation, he turned to her. "We won't be here in the morning."

Lowering himself to the floor again, he said, "Let her watch." Sir growled lustfully as he buried his face in her pussy.

Knowing they had an audience watching added an element of the taboo to their scene.

When Sir spread her outer lips with his fingers and took a long, drawn-out lick, Brie temporarily forgot about the voyeur.

Although she wasn't allowed to make a sound, inside

she was silently moaning, *Oh, Master…*

Sir drew her sensitive clit into his mouth and sucked lightly as he teased her with his tongue. It didn't take long for another orgasm even more powerful than the last to hit Brie.

He then licked her clit as it pulsed against his tongue. She had to bite her bottom lip to keep from screaming out in pleasure.

Brie had no control, unlike Sir, who could take oral stimulation for hours. The minute he'd started teasing her pussy, she was completely at his mercy.

And, in true Dominant style, he showed her no mercy, slowly inserting his thumb into her ass as he continued to suck and lick her sensitive clit.

But this time, just before she was about to climax, he pulled away from her.

Her entire body was left hanging on the precipice, pulsing with desperate need.

Brie held her breath.

She felt crazy with desire. To distract herself, she stared at the woman watching them.

When Sir's tongue returned to her wet pussy, she let out an unintentional moan.

"Tsk, tsk," he murmured, the loud smack on her ass echoing through the empty apartment.

Brie bit her lip again. Of course, Sir knew she enjoyed the way he spanked her. His punishment tonight was acting more as a tease than actual correction.

Still, Brie wanted to impress Sir with her level of obedience.

She stared straight ahead, her eyes focused on the

voyeur's silhouette.

Slowly sliding his finger into her ass, Sir commanded, "Come."

Her body was so primed that it immediately tensed, readying itself for release. She had no control as her thighs started shaking.

A cold chill took over and her nipples hardened against the glass as her body reached release in an explosion of pleasure. Tears came to Brie's eyes because it felt so good.

Sir wasn't done, pressing his tongue against her clit while it was still pulsing as her climax finished. With a will of iron, she stayed quiet and still.

"You taste so good, téa…"

She stared at his reflection in the glass, knowing in every way that he was testing her resolve.

Then he kicked it up a notch, announcing in a gravelly voice, rich with lust, "Your ass calls to me, but that pussy is too damn hot."

Her cry of pleasure caught in her throat when she heard him unzip his pants. She watched Sir's reflection as he got into position behind her and she felt him press his cock into her swollen pussy.

Brie trembled as he pushed his shaft deep into her needy depths. She was so wet and ready, her body had no trouble taking his full length. He thrust hard into her, causing her nipples to rub against the cold glass with each stroke.

When he grabbed her buttocks and forced himself in even deeper, Brie braced herself against the glass, needing to take it hard and fast.

She looked at Sir's reflection as he ramped up, his

strokes solid and powerful. It was erotic to watch him fuck her as her body rocked with the impact of each stroke.

The rough claiming caused another orgasm to crash over her and she heard Sir's masculine groan as her pussy contracted rhythmically around him. Afterward, she gushed with her come.

"Fuck…" he groaned when he felt it.

The orgasm was so intense, it left Brie weak afterward and she struggled to stay steady on her feet.

When Sir suddenly pulled out, her pussy literally dripped with come onto the floor.

He leaned forward, whispering in her ear. "You've got my cock so wet, téa, I'm going to have to fuck your ass now."

Her knees almost buckled when she felt the head of his hard cock pressing against her anus. The fact that she was so wet that he didn't need extra lubricant spoke to how incredibly turned on she was.

Brie was desperate for Sir to claim her.

Closing her eyes, wanting to feel every delicious sensation, she forced her body to relax as she felt his rigid cock opening her up and pushing inside her.

Brie wanted to cry out in ecstasy as he began stroking her tight ass, giving her exactly what she needed.

"You feel too good," he murmured huskily.

Brie nodded vigorously, agreeing one hundred percent with him that it felt too good.

Sir stopped several times to regain control. Those short interruptions made it more exciting because each time he reentered her, her inner muscles squeezed his cock hard, causing exquisite feelings for them both.

"I'm going to come," he growled.

Brie's pussy contracted in pleasure. Her heightened sensitivity was one of her favorite aspects of anal sex. She could feel everything when he came and she *needed* to feel his come deep inside her.

The goosebumps started again when he began pumping his cock hard into her ass. It took everything in her not to cry out and tell him how good it felt when his cock pulsed as he released his seed inside her.

All of it was too much and her muscles tensed again, needing to climax.

"Yes…" he murmured huskily as she came a fifth time with his cock deep inside her ass.

Her muscles milked his cock as she whimpered in pleasure.

When he pulled out, she slowly slid down the glass, no longer able to support herself. Sir knelt down behind her and pulled her against him. The room was silent except for their rapid panting.

The two of them stayed in that position, oblivious to the rest of the world, while they recovered from their intense coupling.

Brie kept her eyes closed, feeling both wonderfully vulnerable and equally protected in his arms.

As a final act of dominance, Sir interlaced his fingers with hers and squeezed her tight against him.

"Mine."

Sir stood up, helping Brie to her feet. She noticed their

voyeur had turned off the living room light, but there was another light on farther inside the apartment. Brie imagined she was making good use of the scene she had just witnessed.

After getting dressed, Brie asked Sir if she could say goodbye to the apartment.

He chuckled softly, "Certainly."

Brie went to their kitchen first. This room had been a source of humiliation, triumph, and love. It was here that she learned Sir didn't eat eggs—or breakfast, for that matter—after her failed attempts at trying to make him an omelet that first morning. But this was also the kitchen where she had finally succeeded in making Sir's favorite dish, Ribollita. In this very kitchen, Sir, the man who hated Christmas, had surprised her with a Christmas scavenger hunt that she would never forget.

Running her hands over all the counters and appliances, she looked to where the table used to be and said in a wistful voice, "I remember all the conversations we had here."

Sir touched her temple and said, "They're all still in here, babygirl."

She nodded, knowing he was right.

Brie headed to their bedroom at the end of the hall. Gone were the gothic ironwork and crimson walls. In its place were completely vanilla walls painted a plain eggshell white with an empty closet devoid of fun toys.

She let out a small sigh. It was in this room that Brie truly came to understand Sir—not only his preferences and many talents but the man behind the Master. It was also in this room that Sir had learned to walk again and reclaim his life after the accident.

So much had happened in here, and now it had all been erased. It was a clean slate for someone else to create memories in.

Brie headed to the baby's room last.

She chuckled, remembering that in the beginning, this room had been a storage room for all her stuff. Sir had not been prepared the night he collared her, but he still insisted that she quit her job at the tobacco shop and start on her first film while she moved in with him.

It had all been a wonderful shock to her.

At the time, Sir told her that he would never have kids and, eventually, the room was turned into a guestroom that Master Anderson, Tono, and Rytsar had all ended up using. But, it finally found its real purpose when Hope graced the world.

Running her hand down the doorframe, Brie held back the tears.

This was Hope's room.

Brie had spent countless hours in here breastfeeding her and rocking her when she couldn't fall back to sleep.

So much of her was tied up in this place…

"No need to cry, babygirl," Sir told her. "Life is out there and we need to pick up our little girl so we can take her home.

Home…

A permanent home where Hope could grow up and have a lifetime of memories.

Brie smiled up at Sir and took his hand. "Yes, it's time to go home."

The Letter

The tranquility of their new lives was shattered when Rytsar received a letter from Russia.

Brie was visiting Rytsar at his beach house so she could give her favorite Russian a little *dyadya* time with Hope. While he played with the baby, Brie entertained herself by throwing a tennis ball for Little Sparrow. Brie threw the ball in the air but when the dog leaped up to catch it, the ball bounced off her nose and rolled under a desk.

She looked at Brie and whined.

"I'm sorry, sweetie," she told the dog, getting down on her hands and knees to look for the ball. When she reached out to grab it, however, she noticed a letter that had slipped behind the desk. She pulled it out and stared at the envelope, intrigued by the flowery handwriting.

Suspecting it was from a woman, she got back on her feet and walked over to Rytsar, who was making Hope giggle with a game of peek-a-boo.

Brie was curious about who had sent it, and asked,

"New secret admirer?"

"I have many, *radost moya*," he answered with a teasing smirk. Shifting Hope over to one arm, he took the letter from her. Rytsar studied the return address and smiled as he tore open the sealed envelope.

"It's from a submissive of mine—a girl I've scened with many times," he explained, chuckling as he pulled out the letter. "She is a feisty one and often needs to be punished."

As he read it, the smile on his face slowly disappeared.

"What's wrong?" Brie asked, now worried.

He shook his head.

Watching him as he read it through again, Brie saw the color drain from his face.

"Is she okay?"

Without answering, he handed Hope to Brie, set the letter on the counter, and walked out the front door, heading toward the beach.

Stunned, Brie stayed rooted where she was and watched him through the large window. Rytsar walked to the water's edge and just stood there, staring out at the ocean.

Her heart raced as she glanced at the letter again. Although she was sorely tempted, she did not pick it up to read it. After her dealings with Ruth, Sir's mother, Brie had learned her lesson about reading letters that were not addressed to her.

Knowing that Rytsar would have handed her the letter if he'd wanted her to read it, she left it where it was and walked out with Hope to join him on the beach.

Once she reached him, she stood beside him in silence.

"Did you read it?" he asked gruffly.

"No."

"Good."

Brie's heart ached, knowing whatever that letter contained had deeply upset him. But not understanding the cause of it was eating her up inside.

"Is there any way I can help?" she offered.

Rytsar put his arm around Brie, pulling her to him as he continued to stare at the ocean in silence. Hope seemed to sense the gravity of the situation and did not squirm as he hugged Brie in his tight embrace.

She laid her head against his chest and could hear his heartbeat—it was racing.

Brie closed her eyes, trying to calm her own heart, which had begun racing, too. Whatever was in that letter had shaken Rytsar to the core.

They stood there for so long without moving that Sir must have noticed from their own home, because he came up behind them and asked jokingly, "Are you having a private moment or can I join?"

When Rytsar turned to meet his gaze, Sir immediately asked, "What's wrong?"

"I'm not ready to talk about it, *moy droog.*"

Sir's expression changed from a look of concern to one of compassion as he placed his hand on Rytsar's shoulder. "I'm here for you, brother."

Brie could feel Rytsar's muscles relax in response to Sir's physical touch. Nodding, Rytsar kissed Hope on the head and looked out at the ocean again.

They stood in silence, both Sir and Brie wondering what could have befallen Rytsar to leave him so bereft.

Brie continued to listen to his racing heartbeat as the waves crashed against the shoreline. She tried to focus on the sound of the waves to keep from totally freaking out.

Finally, Rytsar let out a deep sigh and released his hold on her.

"I have calls to make."

Sir asked him, "What can I do to help?"

Rytsar shook his head. "Nothing, comrade. This is something I must do alone."

"Surely, there is something?" Sir insisted.

Rytsar shook his head sadly, leaving them on the shore as he walked back to his house alone.

Sir turned to Brie. "What happened?"

She frowned, looking at Sir in concern. "He received a handwritten letter from a submissive in Russia. That's all I know."

Sir looked back toward Rytsar's beach house with a worried expression. "I've never seen him like this."

A shiver ran down Brie's spine. She knew the two men had been close ever since college and Sir had seen Rytsar through some particularly violent times.

"I'm scared, Sir…"

Hope started fussing in her arms.

Sir took her from Brie and smiled reassuringly. "There is no reason to be scared. Whatever has happened, we will address it once we know what we're dealing with."

He gave her a quick kiss and started walking toward

their home.

Brie took solace in Sir's ability to compartmentalize a problem and figure out the best solution. It was one of his many talents.

But, when she glanced back at Rytsar's beach house, she couldn't shake the feeling of dread in her heart.

To stay distracted, Brie spent the day cleaning things that did not need cleaning and straightening up everything in the house twice.

Sir finally stopped her. "You are making me nervous, babygirl."

Brie smiled apologetically. "I'm sorry, Sir."

"I think I know what can quiet your mind." He held out his hand to her.

Guiding her toward the couch, Sir commanded she sit down, then left her alone in the room while he went to get something. She wondered what kinky thing he had in mind and was surprised when he returned with their sleeping baby in his arms.

Brie laughed softly as he lay Hope in her arms.

Hope wiggled momentarily without opening her eyes before settling back to sleep. Sir sat down next to Brie, saying, "I find there is nothing more calming in this world than a sleeping child."

He moved his hand down to Brie's stomach, resting it there. "Especially when that child was created out of love."

Brie turned her gaze away from Hope. "And damn hot sex."

"That's something we won't tell her." Sir chuckled, staring down at their child.

Brie grinned. "I wonder how many children are the products of the hottest sex their parents have ever had?"

His chuckle grew deeper as he turned to kiss Brie on the lips. "I say when the time is right, we should see if we can't top number one."

Brie returned his kiss, her entire body thrilling at the prospect of making another baby with him. Baby-making sex with Sir was completely and mind-blowingly hot. "Do you want to start sooner rather than later?"

Sir reached out and caressed Hope's soft hair. "Not quite yet. This little girl deserves our full attention right now."

Brie loved how thoughtful Sir was as a father. He had been afraid that he was too wounded to properly care for a child, but just looking at him staring down at Hope with such love in his eyes was proof enough that he took after his father.

She'd never doubted he would make the best kind of daddy—although she had also suspected he would be overly protective of her. It was going to be interesting to see how that played out as Hope grew older.

"Looking at her brings me joy," he whispered.

Brie gazed down at Hope sleeping so peacefully in her arms and smiled. "Me, too..."

A week later, they still had not heard a word from Rytsar about the letter. Sir reminded her to be patient, but not knowing was killing her inside.

So, when she went on her morning stroll down the beach and saw Faelan's blue Mustang in Rytsar's driveway, she decided to pay Rytsar a quick visit. She figured it would give her a good excuse to see Rytsar and satisfy her curiosity at the same time.

She knocked on his door and was surprised when Maxim answered it. She knew it meant that Titov had returned to Russia, which made her sad because she hadn't had the chance to say goodbye.

"Mrs. Davis is here," he announced formally.

"Enter, *radost moya*," Rytsar called out from inside.

Stepping aside, Maxim let her in with a curt nod.

She saw Rytsar talking to Faelan in the kitchen, and walked over to greet them. "Well, this is an unexpected treat to see you here, Mr. Wallace."

Faelan turned to her. He looked as charming as ever with his twinkling blue eye and that stylish eyepatch. "Good to see you again, Mrs. Davis."

She noticed he was holding a Frisbee in his hand. "Are you giving Rytsar pointers on how to throw that America classic?"

"Actually, I've come to pick up Little Sparrow."

Brie looked at Rytsar, her heart dropping. "Why?"

"I'm leaving for Russia, *radost moya*."

She swallowed hard, trying to keep her tears back. "You're leaving us?"

"*Da.* There is business in my homeland that I must attend to. Thankfully, Wolf Pup has agreed to take Little

Sparrow while I'm gone."

"Sir and I would have been happy to—" Brie began.

"No," Faelan interrupted. "Durov and I have a long-standing agreement. Whenever he leaves, Little Sparrow is mine to look after." He knelt down and rubbed the dog's furry head. "The two of us have a special bond."

The dog wagged her tail enthusiastically, licking Faelan's face with obvious adoration.

"Besides," Rytsar stated, smirking at Brie. "I can't imagine my comrade surviving with a dog in his new house, on top of the *kot*."

Brie giggled to herself, thinking back on all the trouble Rytsar had with Shadow in the beginning. "Still…I'm positive Sir and I could make it work."

"No one is stealing away my time with Little Sparrow," Faelan declared, standing back up. "Isn't that right, girl?"

She ran to the door, staring at the plastic Frisbee in his hand.

Faelan shrugged. "I never could resist those big brown eyes." Nodding to Brie and Rytsar, he announced, "I'll be back in a few."

After Faelan left, Brie turned to face Rytsar. "I'm worried."

He chuckled. "Don't be, *radost moya*. The Wolf Pup may not compare to me, but Little Sparrow likes him well enough."

She knew he was avoiding the real issue by purposely misunderstanding her, but she played along with it, respecting Sir's advice. "I thought you stopped calling him Wolf Pup."

"I did, but the kid insisted. Claimed he missed the nickname—something about it keeping him humble."

Brie looked out the large window as Faelan sent the Frisbee flying through the air and Little Sparrow took off after it.

Todd Wallace never stopped surprising her.

He'd grown into a remarkable man—so different from the boy who had opened the door for her every day in his pursuit of her while she attended the Submissive Training Center.

Faelan was a fighter but, over the years, he'd proven himself not only to be exceedingly brave but also unfailingly loyal. Protecting her from Lilly, then going to Russia to rescue Rytsar and losing his eye because of it…

Rather than retreating into himself after such a significant loss, Faelan had somehow become stronger and more determined. Brie suspected that part of the reason was due to his new girlfriend, Kylie.

Not that long ago, Brie had been certain that Mary and Faelan were meant for each other, and she had worked hard to make it happen.

Faelan even collared the girl but, in the end, Mary broke his heart.

Brie felt personally responsible for that due to how hard she'd pushed the two together, and Faelan had every reason to resent Brie for it—but he didn't.

Following the traumatic breakup, he moved back to LA and threw himself into scening at the Haven, quickly building a reputation among subs and Doms alike.

It seemed funny to Brie now that she'd thought Faelan was extremely arrogant when she first met him.

While it was true that Faelan was confident as a Dom, she'd come to understand he was humble as a man. He'd lived under the immense guilt of having killed one of his classmates in a car accident when he was young. But, it wasn't until Kylie entered the picture that Faelan finally faced his past and was able to move on.

Hearing from Rytsar that Faelan had insisted that he keep calling him the Wolf Pup only highlighted how grounded Faelan truly was.

Brie respected him more for it.

"Faelan is pretty amazing," she stated, watching as he played with the dog on the beach.

"*Da*," Rytsar agreed in a solemn voice, but then he suddenly burst out laughing when Little Sparrow jumped high in the air and caught the Frisbee between her teeth, prancing proudly back to Faelan, tail high.

"He is the only one I trust to care for *Vorobyshek* while I'm gone."

Brie's heart ached on hearing him mention how he was leaving again. "So, how long will you be gone?" She kept her tone light, hoping it wouldn't sound too intrusive.

Rytsar raised an eyebrow. "I know what you are doing, *radost moya*."

She looked at him guiltily, unable to hide her concern any longer.

Letting out a long sigh, he said, "I suppose it's time that I tell you."

"What is it, Rytsar? What's happened that is forcing you to leave for Russia so quickly?"

He put his hand on the back of her neck and

squeezed firmly. "Go get your Master after the Wolf Pup leaves. I will speak to you both then."

Brie nodded, but her stomach was twisting into a knot. Based on his tone, she knew Rytsar was deeply unsettled. Her first instinct was to hug him but she stayed still, responding to the tight hold he had on her neck.

Faelan walked in, his hair windblown by the ocean breeze. He looked relaxed and happy as Little Sparrow pranced in joyfully by his side.

Brie heard Rytsar's quiet sigh and suspected he was already missing the dog even though she hadn't left him yet.

It seemed as if Little Sparrow understood because, when he sighed, she cocked her ear up and ran to him. She started licking his hand, whining softly.

Rytsar let go of Brie and bent down to pet her. "It's time to go, *Vorobyshek*."

Walking over to Wallace with Little Sparrow by his side, he took Wallace's hand and placed it on the dog's head. "*Ostat'sya ryadom*."

Little Sparrow whined but obeyed, staying next to Faelan while Rytsar walked back over to Brie.

"It is best that you go now, Wolf Pup, and spare us both a lengthy goodbye."

"Certainly," Faelan answered, looking at him with compassion.

"As far as my return, I'll contact you as soon as I have a set timeline."

"Take as long as you need, man. You know I like hanging with this girl." Rubbing her head again, he handed the dog the Frisbee. "Hold this."

Little Sparrow gripped it in her teeth and followed him out the door but stopped in the entryway to look back at Rytsar.

"Go," he ordered gently.

Her tail lowered, but she obediently headed out with Faelan as Maxim shut the door.

Rytsar looked at Brie and nodded. "Go get your Master. There is much for us to discuss."

As soon as Brie was out the door, she ran to their house, bursting through the front door, calling for Sir.

He came out of his office looking concerned. "What is it, babygirl?"

"Rytsar needs to talk with us...he's leaving!" she cried.

"Leaving where?"

"Wallace just picked up Little Sparrow so he can fly to Russia."

Sir stood up and took out his phone, dialing it quickly. "Look, the baby is still asleep and I'm unwilling to wait. Can you come here instead?"

Sir hung up the phone and, when he saw the worry on her face, held out his hand to Brie. "I know you are concerned, but what he needs most right now is our support."

He wrapped his arms around her. "Whatever this is, we'll face it together."

Brie nodded, taking comfort in his words.

As soon as she heard Rytsar knock on the door, she rushed to open it.

When Rytsar saw her, he walked inside, cupped her

113

chin in his hand, and gently grazed her cheek with his thumb. There was a wistful look in his eye.

She had to swallow down the lump that was growing in her throat.

Rytsar smiled faintly, then turned to Sir. "It would be best if you both sit down."

Sir gestured to Brie to join him on the couch.

Rytsar stood before them, clearing his throat as he prepared to share his terrible secret.

The serious expression on his face concerned Brie.

"As you may know, I was contacted by a sub I know in Russia…"

Sir nodded. "Yes, Brie told me."

Rytsar took in a deep breath, then let it out slowly before he spoke.

Brie suddenly had the irrational hope that he was playing a trick on them, allowing his sadistic side to wreak havoc on their emotions. But, deep down…she knew whatever he was going to say was about to change all of their lives.

Rytsar rubbed the top of his head in frustration. "I never thought I would find myself in this situation."

When he started to pace, it only served to heighten Brie's level of anxiety, but she and Sir said nothing, giving Rytsar the time he needed to voice this terrible secret out loud.

Stopping, mid-stride, he suddenly turned to face them. "I found out that I'm an *otets*."

Sir looked at him, completely stunned. "You're a father?"

Brie couldn't believe it. "But, when? How is that

even possible when you've been away from Russia for so long?"

Rytsar met her gaze, his expression grave. "*Lisichka* has been raising the child for two years."

"Two years…" Brie gasped.

Based on Sir's own experience with Lilly, Brie was not surprised when Sir followed her question up with a more direct one. "Are you certain the child is yours?"

Rytsar nodded, a pained expression on his face. "Three different tests by three different labs. All have confirmed that I am the father."

He started pacing again, growling under his breath. "I have no idea why she kept the child's existence a secret from me."

"Didn't she explain it to you when you talked to her?" Sir asked.

"*Nyet*," he said, frowning. "She insists we meet in person first."

Brie could barely breathe.

Rytsar was a father…

This new reality was going to rip apart the comfortable world they had just built.

Looking into his tortured blue eyes, Brie could tell he was struggling.

She had to remind herself that this wasn't about them; this was about the child and what was best for Rytsar.

"How do you feel about the woman?" Sir asked.

"*Lisichka* has always been a pleasure to scene with," was the only answer he gave, letting them know he had no feelings for her.

Brie couldn't imagine Rytsar having a child with a person he didn't love—especially when he was such a passionate man.

She looked at him, full of compassion, fighting hard to keep back her tears, unable to speak.

Sir asked the question she wanted to know. "When are you leaving?"

"Tomorrow. I have to see the child for myself."

Brie's heart broke knowing that he was leaving them again—and this time there was a chance he truly might not come back.

Hope began crying in the other room. When Brie stood up to get her, Rytsar commanded gently, "Stay."

The crying stopped as soon as Rytsar walked into the room. Brie soon heard the delightful sound of her giggles.

Brie put her hands to her chest when she realized that Hope was losing him, too.

Their little girl would never understand why her *dy-adya* had suddenly disappeared from her life.

As if Sir could read Brie's mind, he put his arm around her and whispered, "We need to be strong for him and think beyond ourselves and this family."

Brie looked at him, nodding sadly. "I know…."

Rytsar came out bouncing Hope in his arms. When she reached out to grab his nose, he took her grasping hand and kissed it. She was not deterred and grabbed his nose anyway, making him laugh.

"You are going to make a great father," Brie told him, knowing it was true.

Rytsar looked her in the eye. "I hope so, *radost moya*."

"You will," Sir stated confidently.

"So is the child a boy or a girl?" Brie asked, realizing he hadn't mentioned it.

Rytsar grinned proudly. "A boy."

"Another Rytsar in the world!"

He replied with exaggerated sadness, "Poor child."

Rytsar then raised Hope high in his arms, looking up at her lovingly as he spun her around. "Don't you dare forget me while I'm gone, *moye solntse*."

Brie's breath caught and she had to look away to stop the tears from falling.

"Do you know what your future plans are?" Sir asked, putting his hand on Brie's back to calm her.

Rytsar lowered his arms, cuddling Hope against his chest. "Not at this point, *moy droog*. First, I meet my son. Then…I go from there."

"How strange it is going to be to meet your son for the first time at the age of two," Brie said with empathy.

Rytsar growled. "*Da. Lisichka* had no right to steal those years from me."

"No, she didn't," Brie agreed, her heart aching for him.

"If there is anything I can do, brother…" Sir stated, looking at him in earnest concern.

"There is nothing you can do at this point," Rytsar answered. "I need to spend uninterrupted time alone with the boy. I have no idea how a man can make up for two years of absence in a child's life."

"You will find a way, and the boy is still young," Sir assured him. "He may not even remember a time when he didn't have a father, as he gets older."

Rytsar sounded doubtful when he answered, "I suppose it's possible…"

"When are you planning to come back?" Brie asked, dreading his answer.

"I do not know, *radost moya*."

She nodded, her lips trembling, despite her best efforts to keep her emotions at bay.

"Whatever my decision, I will return to discuss it with you both," he assured her with a sad smile.

"We will be here when you need us," Sir stated, getting up to give him a hug while Rytsar still held Hope in his arms.

Brie stood up to join them, wanting to surround Rytsar with their love.

The Power of Gray

Knowing they would both struggle while Rytsar was in Russia, Sir asked Brie to invite Marquis Gray and Celestia over to the new house. "Of all the people I know, Gray will give us the perspective we need on this."

Brie wholeheartedly agreed and immediately called to invite them.

"Of course, we will come," Marquis replied on the phone. "But may I ask if there is a reason for this sudden invitation, Mrs. Davis?"

Brie was glad he couldn't see her blush. "Yes."

"Good to know. We will be there at seven."

It was amazing to Brie that Marquis still played such an important role in both of their lives, especially when she considered the animosity that he and Sir had felt toward one another when she first joined the Submissive Training Center.

As her trainer, Marquis had been very protective of Brie and held it against Sir for breaking the school's code of conduct by scening with her in private. Even after the collaring ceremony, Marquis had ridden Sir hard, holding him to an incredibly high standard.

It had caused Sir to deeply resent Marquis Gray, and yet he still respected the trainer—even during those periods when he thoroughly despised the man.

Marquis was extraordinary. He seemed to have the uncanny ability to see into a person's soul. It made him both fascinating and terrifying to be around.

"Sir, they said they'd come," Brie told him after she had ended the call.

"Good. It will be nice to see them both and to thank them again for taking care of Hope during the move."

Brie smiled. "Yes, and we can finally show them the new house now that we're all settled."

"I think a good Ribollita is in order for our guests," Sir suggested. "Will you assist me?"

"Of course," Brie answered enthusiastically. She loved cooking with him in the new kitchen because it was so spacious, and the beauty of it was only enhanced by the ocean serenading them from outside.

Although Brie's cooking skills had certainly improved through much practice, she preferred prepping the ingredients so she could watch Sir in the kitchen. It was like watching an artist at work.

They had established a wonderful tradition since moving into the new house. Whenever Sir cooked recipes from his childhood, they played Alonzo's music. It reconnected him with his father, and she could see an actual change in Sir as he prepared each dish. While he cooked, Sir became more relaxed and joyful, moving about the kitchen with a smile on his face.

Brie loved that Hope would come to associate cooking with seeing her parents together in the kitchen and being serenaded by her grandfather's violin.

Sir left the Tuscan stew simmering on the stove, filling the whole house with its delicious smell. When their guests arrived, it was the first thing Marquis commented on.

"What an inviting smell."

"A family dish of my father's," Sir informed him.

"And which one of you made it?" Marquis asked, having sampled many of Brie's failures in the past.

Sir put his arm around Brie and answered proudly, "We both did."

"I needn't worry about being poisoned with salt then," he replied, giving Brie a wink.

Brie blushed, remembering the night when she'd ruined the beautiful custard she'd made by accidentally adding salt instead of sugar.

Turning to Celestia, she said apologetically, "I still feel bad about you eating that."

Celestia smiled kindly. "Don't be, Brie. It is a fond memory of mine and a testament to how far you have come."

Celestia had this gentle way about her that always set Brie at ease. In some respects, she was the polar opposite of Marquis, bringing calm and acceptance where Marquis always brought intensity and challenge. Together they were the perfect combination.

"By the way, we brought you a housewarming gift," Celestia said, pulling a square box from her purse.

"Thank you!" Brie smiled at both of them as she

took it. Untying the blue bow, she opened the lid and saw a set of marble coasters with "The Davis Home" etched in them.

Brie teared up. The word "home" had such a wonderful permanence about it.

She showed them to Sir while she wiped her eyes discreetly.

"That was very thoughtful. Thank you to you both," Sir told them.

"It's a true pleasure to see you doing so well as a family," Marquis Gray stated.

Sir looked back at Brie and gave her a charming smile. "On that front we are golden."

Marquis Gray nodded, obviously picking up on what was not being said. However, rather than confront Sir on it, he asked, "Where's that cat of yours?"

"Shadow?" Brie asked.

"Yes."

"Follow me and I'll show you." Brie walked them into the great room where Hope had fallen asleep in her carrier. "You can pretty much find Shadow wherever Hope is. I think it's adorable. It's like Shadow has appointed himself as her personal guardian angel."

Shadow had been staring at the baby, but when Brie mentioned his name, he turned his head toward the group, blinking at them with those big green eyes.

"A remarkable animal," Marquis said.

"Why? Did you become chums while you were watching him for us?" Sir joked.

"In a manner of speaking, yes," Marquis answered, looking fondly on the cat.

As if to confirm his statement, Shadow stood up and walked over to Marquis, rubbing his cheek against his pants leg.

"Wow, Shadow doesn't normally take to people," Brie told him. "Although I can't say I'm surprised he likes you. The two of you have similar stares."

Marquis raised an eyebrow. "Do we, Mrs. Davis?"

Brie nodded, suddenly embarrassed for voicing it out loud. "So...this is the great room. Doesn't it have an amazing view of the ocean?"

"It certainly does, Brie," Celestia agreed, instantly making Brie feel at ease again.

"Let us show you the rest of the house while the Ribollita finishes simmering," Sir suggested. Unlike before, he started with the upstairs first.

Marquis was quick to compliment Brie's new workspace. "I'm glad to hear you are returning to your films, Mrs. Davis. You have a simple and honest narrative that this industry sorely needs."

His rare praise overwhelmed Brie. "Thank you, Marquis. Sir has strongly encouraged me to invest more time in my next project."

Marquis glanced at Sir with approval. "As he should."

"I've always been supportive of Brie's career," Sir stated. "While there have been several setbacks outside our control, there's certainly no reason she cannot commit her time and energy now."

"I quite agree."

"Are you planning to release the second documentary soon, Brie?" Celestia asked.

"To be honest, I'm leaning that way, although I long to do Alonzo Davis justice with a documentary worthy of his talent."

She felt as if she was failing the commitment she'd made to Alonzo, a man she had never met but felt connected to, by returning to the other project.

"There is enough time for everything, if you are patient," Marquis assured Brie.

Those simple words gave Brie profound comfort. "I appreciate hearing that, Marquis.

Sir saved the master bedroom for the last of the tour and smiled as Celestia went on and on about how gorgeous their Italian-themed bathroom was.

"It's nice, but I am noticing a curious lack of BDSM equipment," Marquis stated. "There is plenty of space, yet not so much as a single flogger to be found here."

Sir took Brie's hand and kissed it. "We have an announcement."

Marquis looked him dead in the eye. "Go on."

"We've decided to leave the BDSM community."

Celestia gasped.

Marquis Gray glanced at Brie before stating. "If that is the case, you have done a severe disservice to your sub."

"Are you serious?" Sir scoffed.

"Completely," Marquis said, his dark gaze focused on Sir.

Sir broke under the scrutiny and threw his head back, laughing. "Gray, do you seriously think Brie and I would give up the lifestyle?"

Marquis narrowed his eyes. "Are you making a jest?"

Sir smirked in answer before calling out, "Open. Five-two-one-one-four."

The secret door slowly opened and Sir gestured proudly to it. "We took our example from the Gallants, as well as Master Anderson, and have hidden our playroom from the curiosity of others."

Marquis chuckled, shaking his head as he entered the room. When he saw the bondage table, he crinkled his brow. "Is that...?"

"No, it's a replica."

"Ah..." He nodded thoughtfully. "Oddly appropriate."

"I thought so," Sir agreed, giving Brie a private wink.

Marquis glanced around their well-supplied room. "I must commend you for using the Gallants as an inspiration. They have done an exceptional job maintaining the intimacy of their D/s relationship as full-time parents.

"Oh, this truly is a wonderland, Sir Davis," Celestia commented.

Brie smiled at Sir. "It is a love letter written in physical form."

"It certainly is," Celestia agreed.

Sir gave Brie a look of such tenderness, that she felt butterflies in her stomach.

"On that note, I say we go to the dining room and enjoy the Ribollita."

While they were eating, Marquis complimented the richness of the Tuscan stew before remarking, "As perfect as this all seems, there is something out of balance here that I cannot put my finger on."

Sir sucked in his breath, then glanced at Brie. "Actually, it's the reason we asked you to come tonight."

"Would you rather finish the meal or speak of it now?" Marquis asked, putting down his spoon.

"Naturally, we should finish," Sir said, looking across the table at Celestia. "We cooked this meal as a thank you for caring for both Hope and Shadow during our move."

Celestia smiled gently. "It was our privilege to help, Sir Davis. Your daughter is a delight and, as you have already heard, Marquis made a connection with Shadow."

Marquis looked at them both. "When I officiated your wedding, we vowed to support you as a couple. If you ever have need…" He took Celestia's hand. "…we are always here for you."

"It's deeply appreciated." Sir cleared his throat. "Especially at a time like this."

"Why don't you put your father's music on while we finish the meal," Marquis Gray suggested.

Brie had to keep back the tears when she heard the haunting notes of his violin fill the room. They finished the meal in reverent silence. It truly felt as if Alonzo was with them, infusing them with his presence.

After the meal, they retired to the great room. Brie immediately picked up Hope, holding her close, not looking forward to this painful conversation.

"Tell me what has you troubled," Marquis began simply.

"Obviously, this stays between the four of us," Sir began.

Marquis Gray nodded. "Naturally."

Sir explained what had transpired with Rytsar after receiving the letter from Russia.

Brie spoke up. "We are concerned about Rytsar and want to support him, but we are also facing the possibility of…" She struggled to say the words, "…losing him." Tears welled up in her eyes.

Marquis looked at them both and asked, "Do you have a formal ménage relationship?"

Sir shook his head. "Formal? No. But the three of us fully expected to continue what we had. It was part of our motivation for moving to this beach house."

"We are feeling at a loss," Brie told him.

"Brie and I are seeking the proper perspective going forward. We want to be supportive of our friend, even though we are emotionally bereft."

"It's a natural emotion. However, it can be tempered with a healthy mindset. I assume Durov feels the same?"

"He does, but he naturally feels a responsibility toward the child. I know him well and fully expect him to move to Russia once he returns."

"But…we love him," Brie whimpered.

"Sometimes the greatest expression of love is to sacrifice your own desires for the good of the other person."

Brie shut her eyes, forcing back the tears.

"I do not believe the three of you would continue to be happy now that you know of the child's existence."

"Agreed. The child needs his father," Sir replied somberly. "Although I know this, I am still struggling. Durov has been through hell his whole life, and I have always had his back. I'm afraid this has the potential to be a different kind of hell for him. Stuck in a loveless partnership for the sake of the child...but there is nothing I can do."

"No," Marquis agreed, "there is not. This is his decision to make."

"But I know it has the potential to kill his soul," Sir stated frankly.

"Only Durov can decide what he's willing to sacrifice for the child." Marquis Gray looked at the two of them in concern. "It seems all three of you will be asked to sacrifice for this child."

"Not just the three of us," Brie said, looking at Hope. Brie realized that her daughter was going to lose him, too, and she was sad for Hope.

Brie understood sacrifice. She had faced it once before with Sir in Italy when she had offered to let him go so that he could pursue Isabella. She had believed Isabella was a better match and was willing to step aside for Sir's sake.

It was the hardest thing she'd ever done, but it was done out of pure love.

Now it seemed she was facing a similar situation—except for one thing. She wasn't sure this woman was the best choice for Rytsar. However, she *did* know Rytsar was the best thing for that little boy.

"We will survive this."

"You certainly will," Marquis assured her.

"But I'm still uncertain if that will be the case for Anton," Sir growled. "I can't help feeling this could be a trap."

Marquis laced his fingers together thoughtfully. "Do

you think it's possible that your experience with your sister has clouded your ability to be unbiased in this situation?"

Sir sat back in his chair, folding his arms. "I don't…" He paused for a moment. "Perhaps."

"Your real struggle may be more about yourself than a legitimate concern over Durov's situation."

Brie saw the look of disgust on Sir's face and knew he was directing it at himself. Her heart broke, and she called out to him, "Sir…"

Brie did not miss the momentary flash of darkness in his eyes and she gave Marquis Gray an uneasy look.

Marquis Gray, however, did not seem concerned. "What you need is a clear mind." Looking at Brie, he added, "Your wife knows the power of a good flogging."

To Sir, he said, "I'd be willing to do the same for you."

"A flogging?" Sir seemed thrown by the offer and got up to walk away. "I came to you looking for answers, not a flogging."

Brie held her breath, believing that Marquis Gray's offer was exactly what Sir needed, whether he realized it or not.

"Give me a minute," Sir stated, heading outside.

The three of them watched as he stood on the porch, looking out at the ocean.

"It's fine if you want to leave us to talk to him," Celestia assured her.

Brie shook her head. "No. Sir left us because he needs time alone to think this through."

"You agree it will help?" Marquis asked her.

"Of course. It's exactly what he needs." She glanced back at Sir. "I just hate seeing him in pain."

"I'm proud of him," he stated. "The Thane Davis I knew would not have reached out for help."

Brie nodded. "Sir has changed a lot in the last few years. He isn't willing to suffer in silence any longer."

"That's the sign of maturity."

Brie frowned slightly, her eyes drifting back to Sir. "I wish that his maturity hadn't come at such a high cost."

"We aren't given a choice on what we will face in life, but we *do* get to choose how we react to it. Thane is a prime example of that."

Brie gazed back at Sir, saying with admiration, "He is a perfect example."

"And you, Brianna, are his compliment."

She blushed.

"I've never forgotten the meek girl who walked into the Training Center. I understood your potential the moment I saw you, but it meant nothing until you understood your power and believed it yourself."

Brie remembered how intimidated she had been by Marquis Gray in the beginning. "I appreciated that you always pushed me, Marquis."

"You are a rare pearl." He glanced at Celestia and smiled. "We both feel that way."

"We certainly do," Celestia agreed. "It is easy to help those you admire."

Brie laughed. "You are the ones to be admired."

"There comes a point when the teacher and the student become equals. You are reaching that sooner than you think."

Everyone turned on hearing the door open. Sir walked back inside and stated, "Gray, I have decided to take you up on your offer."

Marquis gave a single nod. "Very well."

Celestia stood up, moving to the baby, who was now awake and opening and closing her hands, wanting to be picked up.

"I'd be happy to watch over her with Shadow," Celestia offered, looking tenderly at the big black cat.

Brie turned to Sir. "Would you want me to be present, Sir?"

He took her hand and pulled her close. "I *need* you there, babygirl."

Brie was deeply touched, remembering there had been a time when Sir would have pushed her away in a moment of weakness.

After the airplane crash, however, all that had changed. She'd seen him at his weakest point, encouraged him through it, and loved him all the more afterward.

It was an honor that he now trusted her in every aspect of his life.

"I see no reason to wait," Marquis Gray stated, standing up to walk over to Celestia, who was bouncing Hope on her lap.

"This may take a while," he warned her.

Bowing her head in acknowledgment, Celestia answered, "I understand, Master." Looking down at the baby she added, "I'm certain Hope and I will have no problem entertaining ourselves."

Sir took Brie's hand as they followed Marquis Gray

into the master bedroom and shut the doors behind them.

"I think it is best if we do it out here, rather than in your playroom. However, the window may prove a problem for us."

In answer, Sir picked up a remote resting on the nightstand and pressed a button. Window shades slowly lowered from the ceiling to the floor, adding a darker but transparent shield between them and the rest of the world.

"We can still look out, but no one can see in," Sir explained.

"Brilliant," Marquis complimented. "May I choose an instrument from your collection?"

"Certainly." Sir called out the code, and told him, "The entire selection is at your disposal."

Marquis Gray nodded and started toward the play-room.

"What should I do to prepare?" Sir asked, his voice sounding uncharacteristically off.

Marquis Gray turned to meet his gaze. "During the session I want you to concentrate on the concept of letting go of the bond that binds you."

Brie noticed Sir stiffen.

After Marquis disappeared into the playroom to pick out a flogger, Sir immediately stripped off his shirt, handing it to Brie, and instructed her to get a pair of sweatpants.

He stripped down to his boxers and traded Brie his clothes for the black sweats. She could feel his anxiety rolling off him, and asked quietly, "Are you okay?"

He glanced at her with a look of uncertainty. "Hopefully, I will be after this, babygirl."

Marquis brought out the flogger he'd given Brie as a birthday gift. He'd made it by using a combination of suede and oiled leather tails. "I designed this flogger for longer sessions, so it will do nicely for what I have in mind."

Sir stared hard at the flogger.

"Are you concerned, Sir Davis?" Marquis asked.

"Not about the instrument itself."

"Ah, it's the process itself that concerns you? It's natural to feel resistant when facing one's inner demons."

Sir frowned. "But I thought I was past that."

Marquis met his gaze. "Some demons are of our own making. They can appear innocuous, yet they have the greatest hold over us."

"I'm not sure what you mean."

"I trust you will."

Nodding to Brie, Marquis Gray asked, "Would you select Mozart's *Lacrimosa* for me?"

After she selected the piece on their sound system, Brie handed Marquis the remote and stood back. She felt nervous for Sir, even though she had personally experienced the healing power of a flogger under Marquis' skilled hand.

Marquis Gray directed Sir, "You will kneel, hands outstretched, facing toward the ocean."

Before he followed Marquis Gray's orders, Sir walked over to Brie. Cupping her chin, he gave her a kiss and said in a gruff voice, "Do not leave."

"I won't, Sir."

He walked over to stand before Marquis. Nodding to him, he turned around and knelt on the floor, his arms spread wide.

"You must connect with the music before we begin."

Marquis turned on the music. The instrumental piece started slowly with a sad undertone but quickly began to build in power—the dynamic rhythm of the piece evoking feelings of angst and torment.

A chill washed over Brie.

She was familiar with this music. Marquis had played the same piece when he flogged her after Rytsar's capture. She remembered the intense pain of that session.

But, in its wake, she had felt free...

While the music played, Marquis warmed up his muscles, swinging the flogger like a knight preparing for battle.

Looking at Sir, her heart bled for him, knowing the pain he was about to endure.

Kneeling on the floor with his arms outstretched, she could see the music was drawing out his raw emotions. But, Sir clenched his hands into fists and then relaxed them several times, fighting against it.

Brie glanced at Marquis and saw that his gaze was intense and unwavering as he quietly observed Sir's struggle.

When the piece ended, Marquis ordered him to stand.

Sir was slow to get back on his feet but kept his gaze straight ahead, his face stoic.

"You cannot fight against this or this session will have no effect," Marquis warned.

Sir lowered his head, looking to the side. After several seconds, he lifted his head again, answering hoarsely, "Understood."

"With each lash, you will dig deeper to find the root of your inner struggle," Marquis instructed. "Do not resist it. Let the pain of the flogger push you continually forward."

Sir glanced at Brie briefly, then nodded. He stared straight ahead to indicate he was ready.

When the music started up again, the intensity of it was so powerful that Sir instantly tensed the muscles in his back.

"Relax," Marquis called out above the music.

Sir nodded, visibly relaxing his muscles.

Marquis moved into position, lifting the flogger to deliver the first lash.

Brie held her breath as she watched the multiple tails hit Sir's back with such force that his muscles rippled from the impact.

Sir let out a grunt but remained still as Marquis delivered the next stroke.

Brie's heart ached as she watched Sir take lash after lash. His silence scared her. She knew he was struggling to let go as Marquis continued, each stroke matching the intensity of the emotional music.

Finally, Sir let out a cry of anguish so primal and raw it sent shivers down Brie's spine. She longed to run and comfort him, but she knew this was a journey he must take on his own.

Glancing at Marquis, she had to swallow the lump in

her throat. The great Master had tears in his eyes as he responded to Sir's inner torment, connecting with him through it, while he delivered stroke after stroke.

Marquis Gray was well known for using the flogger to heal the broken, but seeing him tonight, she realized that his power came at a cost. In order to help Sir, Marquis Gray took on the role of an empath, absorbing that pain. The two men bound were by it.

Swinging the flogger like a sword, sweat pouring off him, Marquis relentlessly pushed Sir toward the precipice.

Brie sank to her knees. She found it heart wrenching to watch.

Let go… she begged Sir silently.

A rumble from deep within his chest burst forth as Sir raised his arms, his fists clenched.

"Do not resist!" Marquis demanded.

The lashes suddenly became even more fierce and unforgiving.

Sir shook his head, tears running down his face as he continued to fight it. Finally, a tortured scream erupted from his lips, causing Brie's blood to run cold.

When Marquis turned off the music, Sir slowly sank to the floor as an unsettling silence filled the room.

"Good," Marquis said, panting heavily as he lowered the flogger and walked to Sir.

Sir's eyes were closed but tears streamed down his face.

Marquis placed his hand on Sir's shoulder and said nothing. They stayed in that position for several minutes until Sir opened his eyes.

"What did you learn?" Marquis asked.

"I have fought for so long to protect my brother." He said it with such sorrow it pricked at Brie's heart.

"I would do anything for him."

"And what will you do now?

"Take a step back, so I can see things clearly."

"Clear sight will prove invaluable as you move forward with Durov."

Sir's head dropped. "But I couldn't bear it if I lost him." Sir swallowed hard. "Ever since college, I have been afraid… And, time after time, fate has tested those fears."

Marquis squeezed Sir's shoulder. "The time to fear is over."

His pronouncement sent a shiver through Brie. She felt as if those words were meant for her, as well.

"Brie…" Sir called out, his voice raw.

When she ran into his arms, Sir pulled her to him. She could feel his entire body trembling.

Brie kissed Sir's sweaty skin all over, grateful Marquis had walked him through to the other side intact.

"What can I do for you, Sir?"

He whispered in her ear, "Be with me."

That night, after his flogging session with Marquis, Brie felt a distinct change in Sir.

Once again, he was in control, trusting his ability to support his friend in whatever capacity he was needed.

It gave Brie the confidence that she could do the same.

Spa Day

Wanting to lose herself in her film, Brie was hunched over her computer as she worked on film edits. But, having been at it for hours, things were starting to blur. Banging repeatedly on the same key, she cussed at her computer in exasperation.

Sir surprised her by coming up from behind and placing his hands on her shoulders.

As soon as she felt the welcomed electricity of his touch, she sat back in her chair and purred. "Ah…that feels wonderful."

"You seem awfully tense," he stated as he massaged her shoulders.

"I'm just trying to edit this piece but my computer is being a butt."

"A butt?" he chuckled. "Is that your way of saying you need a new computer?"

She stared at the screen, frowning. "No. It's really a case of user error. I've been editing this same scene for three days now and it's still not quite right."

"Maybe you need time away."

"Yes…but even if I work on another segment, Lea and Tono's scene will keep eating at me until it's right, and it's wearing me thin."

Sir turned the chair around so that she was facing him. "When I said time away, I meant away from the computer. Why don't you enjoy a spa day and invite whomever you want to join you? It's been a while since you've had time alone with your friends."

It sounded like the perfect distraction.

Brie stood up and then went on tiptoe to wrap her arms around the back of his neck. "How did I get so lucky?" she asked, kissing him on the lips.

"It had nothing to do with you, my dear, and everything to do with your butt." He smirked as he slapped her hard on the ass before grabbing a fleshy handful.

Brie invited Lea and Mary to meet her at a fancy spa in Santa Monica. She really craved spending some time with the two of them, especially after having edited both of their scenes for her documentary recently.

Lea waltzed into the spa first, and let out a high-pitched squeal when she saw Brie. "Hey, girlfriend!"

Brie noticed the other women in the waiting room were giving Lea a condescending stare. That was one thing about LA that Brie didn't like. A lot of people tended to think too highly of themselves and were unfriendly.

She stood up and purposely gave Lea a long hug in the middle of the room, not caring what the other women thought. "So glad you could make it, woman. We haven't had girl time in ages."

"I know! Crazy to think how long it's been."

When they sat down, Lea immediately bumped shoulders with her. In a voice loud enough that the other women would hear, she said, "They say going to the spa is all about loving yourself—but I say the magic wand does a better job."

Brie's eyes widened, caught off guard by the joke, and she burst out laughing.

One of the other women huffed in disgust, noisily snapping open a magazine to make sure they noticed.

It didn't deter Brie and she shoulder-bumped Lea back. "I have to agree, and you don't have to deal with a bunch of stick-in-the-muds."

"Unless you like that kind of kink," Lea added, giggling.

Mary strode into the spa looking like she had a chip on her shoulder. Suddenly, all eyes were on her. Even the woman with the magazine put it down to stare at Mary.

After hooking up with Mr. Holloway, Mary had made a definite mark in the acting world. The rude woman stood up and walked straight over to her. "Oh, my God. Can I have your autograph, Miss Wilson?"

Mary frowned. "Do I look like I'm in the mood to sign a fucking autograph?" Shaking her head, she brushed past the woman and walked over to Brie.

"Hey, Stinks."

Brie had to laugh. Mary fit in perfectly with this kind

of crowd.

"How's life treating you?" Brie asked, scooting over so Mary could sit in between them, protected from any other autograph seekers.

"I'm in a surly mood. Don't ask."

"I hadn't noticed," Lea muttered.

Mary turned to her. "So, how's single life treating you?"

Brie sucked in her breath. Typical Mary, going straight for the jugular.

Lea answered the question with a joke. "Hey, Mary, how are relationships like algebra?"

"I don't have a fucking clue."

"Sometimes you look at your X and wonder Y."

Mary's lips actually twitched.

Lea looked at her knowingly. "Deep down in that dark soul of yours, I know you appreciate the brilliance of my jokes."

Mary laughed. "Tolerate on occasion, maybe, but I mostly just loathe them."

Without missing a beat, Lea turned to Brie. "Did you know Mary uses lemon juice for her complexion? It's the reason she always looks so sour."

One of the other patrons let out a stifled laugh.

Mary wasn't fazed and egged Lea on. "Seriously, that's the best you've got?"

Lea shrugged. "I figured I'd spare you since I owe you after Liam."

"Don't be doing me any favors. I'm used to you being a mosquito, constantly buzzing around and annoying as heck."

Turning her attention to Brie, Mary asked, "So Stinks, any thoughts on if you'll be releasing that documentary anytime soon?"

Brie noticed the woman with the magazine lowering it again to look at them.

"Mrs. Davis, we're ready for you now." A masseuse from the spa gestured to them to follow her.

"Wait…you're Brie from that movie about the sex school, aren't you?" The woman set her magazine down and stood up. "Can I get your autograph?"

Brie turned and walked away without acknowledging the woman, but Mary shot back, "Stop being such a pest and get some class, why don't ya?"

The woman huffed in indignation, but Brie smiled. Good old Mary never was someone to hold back.

The room the masseuse led them to was set with low lighting and had a gentle waterfall trickling into a pool lit by neon blue lights. Inside the pool of blue water swam several bright orange koi. Brie found the beautiful color contrast charming.

All three of them threw off their clothes, having been used to undressing in front of others during their training at the Center, and laid down on their respective tables.

Brie moaned in pleasure as the masseuse poured warm oil on her skin and began easing the tension out of her muscles. "This is the life…"

Lea was struggling to get comfortable on her massage table, complaining, "These damn boobs…as much as I love them, they can be such a pain sometimes."

Brie looked over to see her masseuse discreetly handing Lea a pillow to place strategically under her chest so she was fully supported.

Mary snorted in amusement, resting her face in the padded hole.

Lea sat up on her forearms, momentarily interrupting her massage. "So, a man has to decide which of three women he plans to marry. So, he tests them by giving each of them five thousand dollars to see what each will do with the money.

"The first woman gets a complete spa treatment and makeover to make herself look good for the man."

"Smart choice," Mary agreed lazily.

"The second woman takes her five thousand and buys the man gifts and gadgets he'd like to make him happy."

"Dumb bitch…" Mary responds, sounding bored.

"And the third woman invests the money, making a hefty return on it, and pays back the man his five thousand."

"Brilliant," Brie pipes up, enjoying Lea's little story.

"So, the man is finally ready to decide, and marries the woman with the biggest boobs."

Brie started giggling while Mary grumbled.

"That's just like a man. Fuckers…"

Brie laughed at Mary. "So says the woman who uses her good looks to manipulate men all the time."

"Shut up, you," Mary told her, but Brie heard a soft chuckle coming from her table.

Lea winked at Brie before lying back down on the table, a huge grin on her face.

The three of them lay there in bliss for several

minutes before Mary muttered, "It's nice when the three of us assholes get together."

Both Lea and Brie lifted their heads to look at each other in disbelief.

"So, Mary, what's been up with you?" Brie ventured as she relaxed back onto the table.

"Another film in the works. You know, same-o, same-o," she replied with disinterest. "So…about that documentary. Is it a go or not? I'm set to make the push as soon as you give me the word."

Brie knew Mary was purposely avoiding her question, so she baited her. "If I give you the down-low on my next release, you have to give me more than 'same-o, same-o'."

Mary shrugged. "Fine."

Satisfied with her answer, Brie told them, "Despite my misgivings about a certain producer who shall remain nameless, I *have* decided to release the second documentary and am working on the edits now."

Lea squealed from her table. "Yay! I'm so happy!"

"Mary," Brie asked, "are you okay with your scene with Faelan being used in the film?"

Mary tried to sound neutral, but Brie heard the catch in her voice when she asked, "What did Faelan say?"

"I wanted to ask you first."

"I don't care."

Brie suspected she really did care, but she didn't want to press her on it. "I'm not compromising on this film. This one is going to be exactly how I envision it. I'll be open to suggestions and if I agree, I'll make changes. But, no more cutting out scenes that I love. It isn't fair to the audience when I know they will not only love all the scenes but may benefit from them, as well."

Mary chuckled from her table. "Oh, Brie's getting all badass now. One documentary under her belt and she thinks she can take on the world."

Brie suddenly felt a fire light up inside her and answered. "You bet I fucking can!"

The three masseuses stopped to clap.

Brie felt giddy inside.

"I'm not sure how well that will go over in Hollywood, but I'm willing to go down in flames with you, Stinks."

Brie was stunned by Mary's statement. She knew how much it could cost her career.

Determined to find out more, Brie decided she would grill her once they had moved into the sauna where they could talk more privately.

One second a saint, the next Mary was harping on the masseuse. "Not so hard, damn it! What you are trying to do, torture me?"

Lea immediately piped up, "What did the sadist masseuse say to her client?"

"Just get it over with…" Mary complained, unwilling to guess.

"Nope, that's not it," Lea teased. "The sadist masseuse told her client, 'Let me know if that's too much pressure. I don't want to torture you. That would be an added charge.'"

Everyone in the room burst out laughing—except Mary—which made Brie laugh.

The vibe in the room felt so good, having the three

of them together again. Even though Mary was obvious-
ly hurting, Lea was still recovering from her breakup, and
Brie was dealing with the agonizing uncertainty of
Rytsar, they were definitely stronger together.

When they finally moved to the sauna, Brie didn't
waste any time. "So, Mary, I fulfilled my part. Now it's
your turn."

"Yeah, spill the beans already," Lea urged.

Mary rolled her eyes, took off her towel, and laid it
down on the cedar bench.

"Move."

Brie and Lea moved to the other bench and watched
Mary lay down, taking up the entire bench for herself.
She covered her eyes with one arm while letting the
other lay limply off the bench. She looked as if she were
planning to take a nap.

"Mary, you owe us an answer," Lea complained.

"I know, Lea," she said in a sarcastic tone. "I am just
getting comfortable before I spill my fucking guts to you
people."

That got both their attentions, and they waited patiently for Mary to begin.

She let out a snarky laugh. "I think Greg is cheating
on me. No, I mean he *is* cheating on me."

Brie and Lea looked at each other, neither surprised
to hear it.

"I'm sorry to hear that, Mary," Brie said. "What happened?"

"I don't even know who the cunt is."

Mary let out a tortured sob, which was uncharacteris-
tic of her. When Brie got up to comfort her, Mary

growled. "Not another step, Brie. Sit down or I'm not saying another word."

Sighing, Brie sat back down next to Lea. Mary was hard, but Brie understood that her childhood had been hell. How could she hold her attitude against her? At least Mary was talking...

"How did you find out?" Lea asked.

Mary said nothing at first, but Brie could see that she was trying hard to get the words out. "We've been struggling...you guys knew that. But I never told you what started it."

"No, you've left us in the dark even though we've been concerned about you."

"You know I don't share shit, Brie." She paused. "But...I haven't been able to shake this. I don't fucking know why. I'm just being stupid."

"Let us be the judge of that," Lea told her.

Mary snorted. She didn't remove her arm from her eyes when she said, "Things were good between us. Hell, even better than I'd imagined. Greg was infatuated with me and couldn't get enough of me. We were fucking like rabbits all the time and he couldn't wait to introduce me to all his Hollywood friends. Fuck, it was everything I ever dreamed of."

Her voice trailed off. "I really thought..."

She was silent for several minutes. Brie and Lea looked at each other, feeling helpless, but Mary had banned them from doing anything to comfort her.

"I should have seen it coming," she said with disgust. "The fucking day it happened was magical, like I was flying on some natural high or something. Best fuckin' day of my life. When Greg said he wanted to go out and celebrate, I was all over that shit."

She paused, her breathing coming fast as she fought off her emotions. When Mary spoke again, her voice was cracked. "I went to take a shower and that's when I saw it…" She bit her lip, trying to keep from sobbing.

Mary's voice sounded hollow. "The words were written in the steam on the mirror, 'Fuck me, Master.'"

She let out her breath. "It wasn't my handwriting."

Brie's heart dropped. "I'm so sorry, Mary."

"Fucking the bitch in our own bed, and he didn't even tell me?"

Brie watched Mary's chest rise and fall as she cried silently.

"That's just wrong on so many levels," Lea growled.

Her eyes still covered, Mary nodded, her lips trembling.

"If things hadn't been going so well, I would have been prepared…" Her voice trailed off, and she shook her head. "I didn't have a clue what was really going on…"

Brie sensed there was so much more that Mary wasn't telling them.

"Do you want us to go punch that asshole?" Lea offered.

"No…" Mary groaned. "You two are fucking pussies."

Even though she was seriously hurt, Mary hadn't lost her sense of humor.

Wanting to dig deeper, Brie asked, "Did he tell you why he did such a disrespectful thing to you?"

She started shaking her head violently. "It's too terrible to talk about."

Brie was certain this had to be connected to her childhood. Although Holloway had sent Mary gifts as a child, Brie had often wondered what kind of relationship Holloway had with her parents, especially her mother.

"Does it have something to do with your mother?" she asked.

Mary went stock-still and it seemed as though the air was being sucked out of the room.

"Mary?" Brie prodded after getting no response.

"I can't, Brie. Saying it out loud would destroy me."

"We would never betray your trust," Lea assured her.

Brie laid her hand on Lea's shoulder and shook her head. "Mary, you don't have to tell us, but we want to help you."

Mary finally lifted her arm away from her eyes. They were red from all the tears she'd shed. "I need you to release that film. I want at least one good thing to come from this horror show."

"Why would you choose to stay with him after what he's done? You don't deserve to be treated like that," Lea insisted.

"You don't understand shit, Lea. There is an ugly underbelly to Hollywood and he's a part of it. I don't have any power, but he does." She lifted her chin defiantly. "He thinks I'm his little puppet, but he doesn't realize I'm equally adept at pulling strings."

"I don't think it's wise to play games with the man," Brie warned.

Mary narrowed her eyes. "This isn't about playing

games, Brie. This is about taking all that power he wields in his fucking fist and producing something of value with it. The only reason he gave your first documentary a chance was because of me."

Even though Mary's statement sounded egotistical, Brie had come to believe it was true based on Holloway's actions, so she did not correct Mary.

"He can't see the gems because of all the shit he produces, but I can. We'll get this second film out there, and I'm going to make certain Greg pours everything he has into it. He'll get all the accolades, but that doesn't matter to me. I just want to see the three of us live on in this film no matter what happens to us in the future. And, if it inspires other girls out there, that'll be fucking fantastic."

Lea shook her head and looked at Mary in disbelief. "Forgive my skepticism, girl, but this doesn't sound like the Mary I know."

Mary stared at her with those bloodshot eyes and said in a voice that chilled Brie to the bones, "I'm not that person anymore."

"Is there really nothing else I can do?" Brie begged her, needing to do something more.

Mary stood up, sweeping back her blonde curls, which were heavy with perspiration. Even sweaty, red-eyed, and naked, she looked stunning and powerful. "Yeah, you can get me out of this fucking sweat lodge and treat me to a mani and pedi."

The door opened and a new group of women walked into the sauna, but stopped short and stared at Mary in awe.

She started forward, casually wrapping the towel around herself as they parted to let her pass. Lea and Brie followed behind, looking as if they were Mary's entourage.

Brie would have found it funny if she didn't know about the incredible pain Mary was going through.

Knowing how much Faelan had truly loved Mary, it broke Brie's heart that Mary hadn't loved herself enough to accept it. Now, Faelan had moved on and there was no turning back.

It was up to Mary to navigate this unforgiving world she had thrust herself into. Brie was committed to standing by her and trusted that Mary would find her own happy ending.

Her Warriors

After two excruciatingly long weeks, Rytsar returned to America. Instead of calling, he texted them both to meet him at his beach house.

The fact that he'd chosen to text them worried Brie.

Unfortunately, Sir was at a business meeting in downtown LA, but he immediately called her when he received the text. "I'm leaving here straightaway. I want you to find a babysitter for Hope."

After getting off the phone, Brie took a moment to breathe and try to still her racing heart. They were about to find out what the future held in store for them, and Brie was terrified that what they learned could destroy what they had.

Keeping her voice light, Brie called the Reynolds, Sir's uncle and aunt. Judy answered.

"Hey, I know this is last minute, but do you mind watching Hope for the evening?"

"Of course not, darling. It'll be good for both children to spend time together. Jack and I want them to grow up having regular play dates."

Brie admired Sir's aunt and uncle for adopting Lilly's son, Jonathan. Their love for the child, mixed with the joy they felt about finally becoming parents, was a beautiful combination. In that kind of environment, Brie had no doubt that Jonathan would thrive.

Brie gathered all the baby paraphernalia required for a long stay, then packed extra, just in case. To help ease her nervousness while she waited, Brie picked up Hope and bounced her as she paced around the house.

When Judy pulled up, Brie ran outside and gave her a spontaneous hug.

The older woman chuckled. "Well, thank you."

"I just appreciate you so much, Judy."

Judy blushed. "Aren't you a sweetheart?"

As they were piling all the stuff into the van, Sir pulled in and parked his car. When he got out, he was the picture of calm.

Smiling tenderly at his aunt, Sir walked over to her and gave her a hug. "It's good of you to do this."

Judy smiled up at him. "As I was telling your sweet wife, it does our hearts good to have the little ones playing together. No trouble at all."

Sir secured the car seat into the van and took Hope from Brie's arms. "Now, you be a good girl for my auntie."

Brie kissed Hope on the forehead before Sir buckled her in. She then handed Judy the insulated bag with her milk. "I gave you extra, just in case."

"Thank you, dear—" Judy stopped, a broad smile spreading across her face.

Brie looked in the car and saw Jonathan reaching over with his little hand, trying to touch Hope. Hope stared at him in wonder, reached out a tentative finger, and giggled when their fingers touched.

"Isn't that just beautiful?" Judy cried.

"It truly is," Sir agreed.

Judy laughed. "I failed to understand how exhausting parenting could be, but seeing moments like this makes it so worth it."

"Yes, it does," Brie said, giving her another hug.

"I'll keep in touch, but it's entirely possible it might end up being an overnight stay," Sir warned her.

"Actually, Jack and I would prefer that," she told him. "With it being such a long drive, it's easier to keep her overnight. Plus, it allows the kids to spend more time together."

Brie waved and smiled as Judy pulled out, but as soon as the van was out of sight, Brie turned to Sir. "I'm nervous."

He nodded. "I'd be lying if I said I wasn't, as well."

"I'm worried because Rytsar texted instead of calling."

"I found that odd, but there's no need to speculate. We can head over now. I'm not going to waste time changing out of my suit."

Brie nodded, anxious to see Rytsar, but reluctant to face whatever news he had.

It was obvious that Sir could read it on her face because he took her hand as they walked over to Rytsar's house.

"We are his support," Sir reminded her as they

walked up to the door.

This isn't about us. This is about Rytsar, she repeated to herself.

Brie was aware that everything she said or did would have an effect on him, so she was determined not to do anything that might have the potential to hurt him now or in the future.

Sir gave her hand another squeeze before he rang the doorbell.

"Come in, *moy droog!*" Rytsar yelled from the other side of the door.

When they entered, Brie was relieved to see Rytsar smiling. He came over and gave each of them a hug. "Thank you for coming."

"Of course," Sir replied. "We arrived as soon as we could."

"I have news."

Ever the sadist, he drew the moment out.

"And your news is…?" Brie asked.

"The boy is the spitting image of me as a child."

Brie actually smiled, finding the idea of a tiny Rytsar running around in the world thoroughly charming. "Did you take a picture together?"

"I did," he said, pulling out his cell phone and swiping through the photos to show her.

Brie couldn't help but smile when she saw a shot of a little chubby-cheeked boy with big blue eyes pressing his cheek against Rytsar's manly jaw.

The resemblance between the two was striking.

Staring at the photo, Brie could imagine Rytsar at that age. It was horrifying to think anyone could hurt such a sweet little child. She looked at Rytsar with fresh compassion, wishing she could have been there to stop the abuse he suffered as a boy.

"Did you fall in love with the little boy the moment you laid eyes on him?"

Rytsar's smile faltered slightly. "The truth is…*radost moya*, I am still adjusting to my new role."

Brie couldn't imagine his emotional shock at finding out he was the father of a two-year-old. Rytsar had never wanted to be a parent, which only made this situation worse.

"How were things between you and the mother?" Sir asked.

Rytsar bobbed his head slightly when he answered. "Sasha is…anxious to become a family."

That was the first time Brie heard the woman's given name, having only known her by her pet name. For some reason, hearing it made things that much more real for Brie.

"How do you feel about that?" Sir asked him.

Rytsar turned his head to look out the window at the ocean. "I am determined to do right by this boy. He will know the love and support of his father."

Having experienced unspeakable cruelty and abuse under the hands of his own father, it was only natural that Rytsar was determined to give this child what he had never known.

Although it broke her heart, Brie understood and respected him for it. "You will be the best kind of father."

He nodded, grateful for her encouragement.

"What reason did Sasha give for keeping the child a secret for so long?" Sir asked him.

Rytsar frowned, looking grief-stricken. "She is well aware of my feelings about having children and did not think I would accept the boy."

Brie's eyes narrowed. She was angry at Sasha for blaming Rytsar for her silence. "How dare she put that on you! She should have told you the moment she knew. It wasn't her decision to make."

"I like your fire, *radost moya*, but whether I am partially to blame for her silence or not is irrelevant at this point." Rytsar gave her a pained look. "The boy needs me."

Brie closed her eyes. She knew Rytsar would move Heaven and Earth for this child. His passion and loyalty were the very things she loved about him.

Her heart ached, certain now that he was going to leave them.

Sir cleared his throat, voicing the question out loud. "So, you are determined to move back to Russia, then?"

"How can I not and still be a true father to the child?"

"Couldn't they move here?" Brie asked hopefully.

Rytsar smiled but shook his head. "Sasha will not leave her family, and insists our son grow up in Russia." He inclined his head toward her, adding, "Which I can't fault her for. I love my motherland."

Sir stared thoughtfully at Rytsar. "Brother, you must do what is best for you and your son. Brie and I will support you in however you need us."

It felt like the ax had finally fallen and Brie struggled

to breathe.

He was leaving…

When Rytsar turned to face her, Brie swallowed down her sorrow, gracing him with the smile he deserved. "We'll just have to come to visit you in Russia."

Rytsar held his arms out to her.

Brie walked into his embrace, resting her head against his muscular chest. But, once there, she felt the immensity of his sorrow and could no longer hold back the tears.

Rytsar was leaving them and the weight of it was crushing her soul…

"I will miss you," she sobbed.

Rytsar didn't reprimand her for crying. Instead, he held her even tighter. "Shh…*radost moya*…shh…"

When she couldn't stop crying, he lifted her chin and gently kissed the tears from her cheeks before pressing his wet lips against hers.

The profound connection in that kiss instantly dried her tears.

When he broke away, Rytsar gazed at her tenderly. "Better?"

She only nodded, not trusting herself to speak.

"I will not be leaving immediately. I need time to prepare."

She gave him a sad smile, grateful to hear it.

Sir had watched the entire exchange. Even though Brie knew he was determined to let Rytsar go, she also knew it didn't make the pain of his leaving hurt any less.

Looking at the two of them, Sir stated in a gruff voice, "I think a session between the three of us is in order."

Rytsar met his gaze and nodded in agreement.

When he looked back at Brie, he had a wicked glint in his eyes. "How would you like to revisit our first session, *radost moya*, for old time's sake?"

Her heart skipped a beat. She remembered the cabin in Russia when Sir had surprised her by inviting Rytsar to join them in their first threesome.

Memories of that night still made her wet.

Brie bowed her head at Sir. "If it would please you. Sir."

He smirked when he answered. "Naturally, téa."

Tingles of excitement coursed through her body on hearing him call her by that name.

In quiet tones, Rytsar spoke to Sir in Russian.

Brie tried to follow the conversation. She had gotten pretty good at basic Russian with Rytsar patiently teaching her his native tongue and Sir letting her practice with him every night.

Although she couldn't quite catch what the two men were saying, she didn't miss the look of lust in Sir's eyes when he answered Rytsar with a throaty, "*Da.*"

Rytsar turned to Brie with a wild gleam in his eyes, shouting, "*Bezhat!*"

She backed away from him, knowing he had commanded her to run, but it wasn't until he lunged for her that she understood he was serious.

Her heart pounding in her chest, she looked at Sir and saw the same wild look in his eyes.

When both men started toward her as one unit, she suddenly understood what was happening. They didn't want to relive that first time in the cabin.

No…

This was her warrior fantasy being played out. Only, instead of one warrior wanting to claim her—she had two.

Brie immediately kicked off her sandals and turned, bolting toward the door. She flung it open with an excited squeal and she raced out of the house with both of them pursuing her.

Feeling the thrill of the chase, she ran as fast as she could down the sandy beach, trying to stay out of the reach of both men. She remembered how quickly Rytsar had captured her the first time and was determined not to be caught so easily this time around.

She could sense Sir and Rytsar drawing nearer and felt chills when one of their hands brushed against her skin as he reached out to grab her.

Remembering that the waves had tripped her up last time, Brie did her best to keep close to the edge of the shore on the firmer wet sand without getting too close to the water's edge. She looked back and saw they were starting to fall behind, slowed down by their restrictive dress shoes.

Brie smiled to herself but couldn't afford to waste the breath to laugh while running at full speed. It felt great to be in the lead!

Unfortunately, it didn't take long before her lungs began to burn.

Slowing down momentarily was enough to give her pursuers the advantage. Brie cried out when she felt the tight hold of Sir's hand gripping her arm. She twisted around, trying to free herself, only to feel Rytsar wrap his arms around her waist as he carried her toward the water and flung her into the ocean.

She was hit by a wave as she scrambled back to the safety of the shore. An intoxicating thrill of fear took over when Rytsar grabbed both her feet and pulled her to him.

Brie let out a terrified scream when he flipped her over and Sir held her down by her wrists. Rytsar crushed her body with his weight.

She gasped for breath as another wave swirled around them and she looked up into her captor's intense blue eyes.

There was a hint of fierceness in his gaze that caused her heart to race even more. Rytsar was a dangerous man, capable of great violence, but he was also a man of extreme passion and fierce love.

No matter how savage his soul, Brie would always trust him.

He leaned down and bit her neck while Sir tilted her head to get better access to her lips, claiming her mouth. His lips tasted of salt from the ocean water.

Brie was overwhelmed by the sense of helplessness caused by Rytsar's teeth bruising her skin and Sir's tongue ravaging her mouth. It was so fucking hot, knowing both men desired her—an exhilaration she never grew tired of.

The fact it was out in the open like this made it that much more arousing for her.

Brie realized she still needed to play the role of a frightened maiden, so she struggled against them. "No, no, no…"

Rytsar's eyes widened, his wicked intentions easy to see as he stood up and grabbed Brie, flinging her unceremoniously over his shoulder before starting toward his beach house.

Sir walked behind, staring at her hungrily.

I bet he wants to nibble some Brie, she giggled to herself.

Struggling not to smile, she had to turn her head to keep her composure. That's when she noticed three women in the distance staring at them, their phones held out in front of them.

Not wanting to relive the "Faelan Incident" again, she broke out of character momentarily, waving at the ladies with a big smile on her face as she bounced against Rytsar's back with her ass in the air.

He slapped Brie's buttocks for good measure, making her yelp before she broke out in giggles.

Brie watched the women put their phones down and talk amongst themselves. Hopefully, the police would not visit them like they had the first time when Faelan thought she'd been kidnapped.

Once they were safely inside and the door was locked, Rytsar set her down on the floor and placed his hand on the back of her neck in a possessive way that sent chills through her. He then ordered Maxim in Russian to get the rest of his men.

Maxim immediately left, returning with three more men from Rytsar's entourage. Rytsar left her alone with the four bodyguards, ordering them to watch her, while he and Sir excited the room.

The four men stood with arms crossed, staring at her.

She couldn't help feeling vulnerable and uncomfortable under their intense gazes, and it made Brie smile to herself.

She had to hand it to Rytsar. He was an expert at evoking the emotions associated with her favorite fantasy—a captured girl, frightened by the fierce warriors around her.

In her original fantasy, she had a rival warrior who had fought to claim her, but in this version, the two warriors were friends and planned to claim her at the same time.

However, as a virgin, she knew such an act should cause her great fear, no matter how handsome her warriors were.

Brie knew it would be easy to fall into the comfortable dynamics of their long-term threesome, but tonight Rytsar and Sir were role-playing with her, and she wanted to make certain she played her part well.

Brie's desire was to fully embrace this gift that they were giving her, so she closed her eyes and refocused her thoughts.

As she plotted out a new version of her fantasy, she found it amusing that she hadn't really changed since her days at the Training Center. She still needed her fantasies to be detailed, and the people who populated them had to have interesting backstories.

Rather than filtering herself, Brie allowed her imagination to run wild...

I've lived alone with my parents ever since we left the safety of Pennsylvania to stake a claim in the West. We'd lost my oldest brother to dysentery during the arduous trip, only to lose my other brother to a snakebite once we'd arrived.

He was off hunting for jackrabbit when a rattler bit him. I will never forget his horrifying scream as he died in my father's arms...

This place has cost us everything that mattered to us, but I've been determined to help make something of this farm to honor my brothers' memories.

Through blood and sweat, and against all odds, the three of us have created a thriving farm and a future for ourselves. But, my pride in our accomplishments is tainted by the fact that I have no one of my own—and it's beginning to weigh heavily on my soul.

My parents have agreed to hire help so I can start life of my own but, just when my dreams are within my grasp...

Our homestead is targeted by a raid.

My father sees the men on horseback first and orders me to run back to the house and hide.

Instincts kick in and instead of running into the house, I run past it, making a beeline for the safety of the creek.

I don't hear screams or war cries—only silence and the crackling of burning wood as I shake uncontrollably in my hiding place. Soon, the smoke swirls in the air around me. I send up silent prayers for my parents, terrified they might already be dead.

After what seems an eternity, I'm certain the warriors are long gone and emerge from the safety of my hiding place to check on my parents. I'm frightened of what I will find.

As I climb the embankment, I suddenly stop cold.

There are two warriors on horseback staring straight at me as if they've known I was hiding there all along.

Even though I know there is no escape, fear takes over and I turn to bolt. I hear the men jump off their horses and hit the ground, and it spurs my flight instinct. With the agility of a deer, I spring up and weave my way through the brambles next to the stream, but it is not enough and soon I feel their hands on me.

I scream as I fall to the ground. One restrains me with the weight of his body while the other secures my wrists above my head. I struggle against them, afraid for my life, and cry out for help that I know will never come.

When I meet the gaze of one of my captors, the intensity of his stare makes me mute. It's as if he can see into my soul.

I'm defenseless when he leans down and bites me on the neck as the other presses his lips hard against mine.

I do not know what kind of dark magic they possess but, for some unfathomable reason, my body responds to their dual embrace. The bite relaxes me while the kiss draws out an internal fire I have never known.

I whimper, scared that they will take me here.

But, they do not.

Instead, they release me. One ties my hands behind my back, while the other lifts me up and carries me to his horse.

I look back at my home as they start out. I am relieved to see my parents holding each other as they watch the house and our barn burn to the ground. I try to cry out to them, but the warrior swiftly covers my mouth and growls a warning.

The raiding party has claimed our livestock and burned down our homestead but, mercifully, my parents are alive.

Unwilling to jeopardize their lives, I stay silent as the warrior kicks his horse, sending us off in the opposite direction...

Now that Brie was in the right headspace, she opened her eyes, accepting the intense gaze of Rytsar's bodyguards as she waited for her warriors to return.

When the two reappeared, she saw they were dressed only in leather pants, their muscular chests enticingly bare.

Brie glanced at them, biting her lip nervously. She was finding it difficult to hide how completely turned on she was. Her nipples stood at attention and were clearly on display through her thin, wet clothing.

The two men spoke to each other in low tones of Russian as their eyes traveled brazenly over her body. Brie had to translate everything they were saying in her head, which added an interesting element to the scene.

Along with their words, Brie used their facial expressions and the tone of their voices to discern the meaning behind what they were saying.

It was obvious to her that they had already discussed how the scene would play out, but there was something different in the tone of their voices and the way they were looking at her that made her heart race.

Brie had a feeling that in this scene, they would challenge her with something completely new, and the idea of that made her extremely wet.

Rytsar produced a knife and made quick work of Brie's wet clothes and panties, leaving her standing naked before them.

Now that she was fully invested in her virginal role, Brie looked down at the fragments of her clothing, and blushed.

When she felt Rytsar's fingers graze her skin, she actually shivered.

No one had ever touched her intimately before…

When Sir joined him, she closed her eyes. Having

two men caress her naked body was both frightening and strangely exciting at the same time.

Their touches were featherlike, not rough as she had expected, causing goosebumps to rise on her skin. Those intimate touches were igniting a longing—a deep, unfamiliar ache—at the core of her being.

The butterflies started when Sir suddenly picked her up and carried her toward Rytsar's bedroom with the four men following behind.

Brie had a moment of real panic. She'd never taken six men at one time, nor did she want to.

To her relief, Rytsar barked an order and the four men headed outside, splitting up to guard the perimeter, with their backs to them.

Brie giggled to herself, realizing the guards were there to prevent another misunderstanding with the authorities.

Sir carried her to the center beam in Rytsar's bedroom, setting her down beside it. Staying true to her role, Brie whimpered when Sir produced a leather tie and grasped her wrists.

Her heart fluttered as he stared at her with the same melt-worthy look he'd given her the day they first met.

Her body could not deny the natural chemistry they shared as he secured her hands behind the pole, and she felt a trickle of wetness between her legs.

Sir stepped back and stood next to Rytsar, the two of them staring at her hungrily.

Brie shivered, noticing the sexual energy in the room seemed heightened and a little dangerous.

The two men started out with nibbles and kisses, loving Brie's body with their lips while grazing her bare skin with their teeth.

As a virgin, she naturally tensed at first, unused to the intimacy of the contact, but her body soon gave in to the sensual feel of their mouths.

When both men grasped her breasts and started sucking on her nipples at the same time, she felt a gush of wetness between her legs.

Brie was completely entranced by their dual attention.

That's when her warriors switched things up on her. Brie held her breath when their hands traveled to her pussy at the same time. One of them rubbing her clit while the other swirled his finger around her wet opening, teasing her.

She closed her eyes as he slowly penetrated her with his finger. In her mind, it was her first time—with all those feelings of how new and strange it felt to have a man's finger inside her.

With the focused attention on her clit added to it, Brie had no chance of controlling the climax that crashed over her. Both men grunted in approval when her pussy started pulsing with her first orgasm.

Rytsar whispered sexy Russian words in her ear while Sir ravaged her mouth with his tongue, helping to prolong her orgasm.

Oh. My. God.

Already flying high, she whimpered in pleasure when Rytsar nuzzled her ear before biting down on it lightly. He growled possessively, murmuring something she did not know the meaning of, but what he said instantly set her heart racing.

Brie was surprised when he untied her wrists and picked her up, taking her to the bed. Apparently, there would be no fucking on the floor this time around.

Goosebumps rose on her skin as she lay there with both men staring at her, the impressive state of their arousal clearly outlined in their pants.

They wanted her.

Brie watched with bated breath as the two stripped in front of her, showing off their rigid cocks. Based on the hardness of their erections, whatever they were planning had both men seriously turned on.

She watched as Sir picked up a tube of lubricant and liberally covered his cock with it. After wiping his hands, he threw the towel on the floor and stared at her. The wildness in his eyes made Brie shiver.

Climbing onto the bed with the grace and focus of a predatory cat, he came to claim her.

But the instant he started to spread her legs, she remembered her role and balked, trying to escape. Sir was ready for it and held her down firmly as he positioned himself between her legs.

Brie liked the sexy thrill of being forcefully taken and struggled even more so that his grip became even tighter.

She fully expected Sir would force his cock into her ass, but he surprised her by thrusting into her pussy. She cried out, taking the full length of his cock in that first stroke.

Sir looked down at her possessively, his gaze captivating her as he claimed his young virgin. Brie threw her head back, giving in to his lust, her pussy *needing* his forceful possession.

She screamed out in passion when he started fucking her hard and deep. She'd expected he would start out slow, but Sir was challenging her body with forceful strokes—and she loved every minute of it.

Brie was already on the edge, feeling the telltale signs of an impending orgasm as he rammed his cock repeatedly against her swollen clit as he fucked her. When he commanded she open her eyes and she met his gaze, she felt a jolt of electricity pass between them. Coming a second time, she whimpered in pleasure.

Sir groaned with satisfaction as her pussy milked his shaft with a powerful orgasm.

Overcome by the intensity of it, Brie lay there panting. She was surprised when Sir wrapped his arm around her, rolling over so she was now on top. She looked down at him, tempted to grind her sensitive pussy against his hard cock even though she was supposed to be playing the part of a virgin.

She suddenly felt Rytsar's hands on her as he repositioned her on Sir's shaft so that she was facing away, in a reverse cowgirl position.

Rytsar moved off the bed, his eyes laser-focused on her as he grabbed the tube of lubricant and coated his shaft with it. He wore a mischievous smile.

Brie watched in breathless anticipation, wondering what he was about to do.

Wiping off his hands, he tossed the towel with a low chuckle. There was no doubting that he had wicked intentions.

"*Radost moya…*" he said huskily as he climbed onto

the bed.

Brie felt Sir's hands pulling her backward. She slowly laid back, her back resting against Sir's chest with her legs wide open.

Rytsar settled between her legs and began petting Brie's slick pussy and teasing her clit, with Sir's cock inside her. Before she knew it, he had her hips bucking as her pussy gushed with watery come.

He licked his finger with a satisfied grunt.

Changing his position, Rytsar stared at her lustfully as he pressed the head of his shaft against her opening, demanding access.

Brie gasped and shook her head.

He nodded slowly.

Brie now understood the reason Sir had coated his shaft in lubricant. They wanted her to take them both at the same time, claiming a part of her that she hadn't expected to give them—like the innocent in her fantasy.

Her nipples contracted into tight buds out of genuine fear. "I can't…"

The gripping fear she felt now was reminiscent of her first scene with Rytsar, only this time, what they were asking of her was so much greater.

Not a man to take no for an answer, Rytsar leaned forward, sucking on one of her nipples as he gazed up at her, his blue eyes burning with desire.

Brie knew this was her decision. She could call out her safeword and end this now, or she could give in to their desire.

For a submissive, there was something powerful in giving away a part of herself she'd never given before.

This is my gift to them.

Brie consciously relaxed in Sir's arms, appreciating the tight grip of his hands on her arms and the fullness of his shaft wedged deep in her pussy.

Rytsar's eyes glowed with fiery lust, knowing she'd made her choice.

Moving back into position, he pressed his cock against her opening and began to push into her.

Brie felt the chills as she surrendered her body to him. This was like the challenge of taking Boa's huge shaft but on such a greater scale.

She slowed her breathing as she forced her body to relax, her pussy lips stretched wide to accommodate both shafts.

It didn't seem possible that she could take even the head of his cock, but Rytsar was patient, taking his time as he slowly sank deeper into her.

Brie cried out when the discomfort almost became too much.

"Shh...shh..." Rytsar murmured, leaning down to graze his teeth against her skin, before biting down on her neck. His bites had an erotic effect on her and her body opened farther for him.

Brie had to remind herself to breathe when Sir and Rytsar began moving as one, starting with shallow strokes.

She looked into Rytsar's eyes as the two men claimed this part of her.

Giving in to their desire was extremely arousing. As they moved inside her, Brie felt pleasant electrical sparks radiating from her pussy.

"Yes! Oh, my, God, yes!" she cried as she started to float, losing herself in the glorious feeling.

It didn't take long before both men reached the edge, the intensity of the stimulation proving too erotic. They cried out in unison as they climaxed inside her. Spread so incredibly tight, Brie could feel every pulse as Sir and Rytsar began to pump their seed deep into her.

Brie about lost her mind feeling both men come inside her at the same time. She screamed out in pleasure and pain—her pussy completely and utterly filled—as her inner muscles clamped around their shafts in one final, orgasmic contraction.

Submissive bliss…

Afterward, she lay in between them with a huge smile on her face.

"Did you enjoy that, *radost moya*?"

"Da," she said, her lazy smile growing bigger. "I am a very happy girl."

Sir nuzzled her ear and whispered, "You look beautiful when you fly, babygirl."

It was then that Brie understood that as much as this had been her gift to them, this had been their gift to her.

Lunch Is On Me

When the doorbell rang, Brie called out to Sir, "Are you expecting anyone?"

"No," he answered from his office.

Brie walked to the door, curious if Rytsar had come for a quick visit. She looked through the peephole but saw nothing, not even a package. Shrugging, she started to walk away when the doorbell rang again.

Running to the door, she peeked through the hole. This time, she saw a black cowboy hat.

"Master Anderson!" she cried, throwing open the door.

He tipped his hat and smiled at her. "Hey, little lady, you wouldn't happen to know where my buddy Thane has disappeared to?"

"Is that Anderson I hear?" Sir called out.

"It is!" she cried happily, thrilled he had come for a visit. Stepping to the side, she said in a formal voice, "Please come in," but she couldn't stop grinning as she walked him into the great room.

Sir stepped out of his office, looking as pleased to see Master Anderson as she was. "Well, this is an unexpected surprise."

"I figured since I drove down here specifically to see you, I might as well stop by," he joked.

Sir gave him an amused smirk. "I'm certainly glad you did."

He slapped Sir on the back. "It's been a while, buddy."

"Too long."

Hope started crying, having been woken from her nap by their banter. Brie hurried to get her, excited to show off how much their little girl had grown.

When she returned, she asked Master Anderson, "Isn't she the cutest?"

"Honestly? She just looks like a baby to me," he answered, chuckling.

Already knowing his answer, she asked teasingly, "Would you like to hold her?"

He looked down at Hope and shook his head. "I'd rather not, no offense."

Brie giggled. "She doesn't bite, Master Anderson."

"No, seriously. I'm happy not holding the baby."

He may have thought he was off the hook, but Sir spoke up, "Nonsense." Taking Hope from Brie's arm, he forced his friend to hold her.

Brie smiled to herself, seeing just how uncomfortable Master Anderson looked holding their little girl, his arms stiff and at awkward angles. He was obviously not a natural when it came to babies, and when Hope moved in his arms, he got a terrified look on his face and tried to hand her back.

Sir shook his head, clearly amused by Master Anderson's discomfort. Taking pity on him, he did show Master Anderson how to hold her, placing Hope against his chest and positioning his hands to give her adequate support.

The broad-chested cowboy looked adorable holding their little girl. Hope was fascinated by him, her mouth open in a perfect "O" as she stared up at the black cowboy hat on his head.

For his part, Master Anderson looked totally out of his element, which made it even more precious to Brie.

That's when Shadow sauntered into the room, heading straight for Anderson.

Master Anderson followed the cat with his eyes, looking at him distrustfully. "What is that cat doing?"

"He's Hope's guard cat," Brie informed him.

Master Anderson tried to shoo him away with his foot, but Shadow would not be deterred.

The cat surprised all of them when he suddenly tackled Master Anderson's leg. Grabbing it with both front paws, Shadow started sniffing his pants, twitching his tail excitedly.

"What the hell?" Master Anderson complained, balancing on one leg as he shook the other, trying to get the large cat off, while still holding Hope.

It was the funniest thing Brie had ever seen and she covered her mouth, trying not to laugh.

"Don't drop the baby," Sir warned.

Master Anderson stopped struggling and stood still with Hope in his arms and a cat glued to his leg, looking at Sir with a chagrined expression. "What did I ever do to deserve this?"

Brie cooed. "I think Shadow must smell Cayenne and the babies."

"That's just great," Master Anderson huffed. Handing Hope back to Sir, he said, "Take your baby back while I get this damn beast off my leg."

Brie watched with amusement as he wrestled unsuccessfully with Shadow to get him off. But, the cat just extended his claws and dug in deeper, determined to stay.

Wanting to help Master Anderson, she said, "Why don't you give me your shirt?"

He looked at her strangely, but not a man to miss an opportunity to bare his chest, Master Anderson whipped it up and over his head, handing it to her.

Brie smiled as she knelt on the floor and let Shadow take a whiff of his shirt. Slowly, the big black cat retracted his claws and jumped off Master Anderson's leg, rubbing his cheek against the soft material of the shirt, purring loudly.

Laying it on the floor, Brie took a step back.

Shadow stood on the shirt, kneading the material with his claws before curling up and lying down on it.

"Aww... Shadow misses her."

"Don't be fooled, young Brie. I know exactly what that black bastard wants."

"What?" she asked, giggling.

"He wants to defile my little girl again."

Master Anderson had never forgiven Shadow for making Cayenne pregnant, but it was obvious to Brie that Shadow and Cayenne were meant for each other. There was no denying that they made beautiful babies together.

"How are the kittens?" she asked.

Brie loved the look of tenderness and pride on Master Anderson's face when he told her, "They are a kick. Never cease to keep me laughing."

She grinned. Even though Master Anderson resented Shadow for making passionate cat love to Cayenne, there was no doubt he was thoroughly enjoying the fruits of their labor.

Master Anderson did not appreciate seeing Shadow love on his shirt and glanced away uncomfortably.

He let out a long whistle. "Holy shit...pardon my language, young Brie...but that is one impressive kitchen you two have."

They walked into the kitchen so he could check it out. "These counters are truly inspiring."

Glancing at Brie, he raised an eyebrow. "I suddenly have a hankering for lunch."

Sir smirked. "Are you offering to make it?"

"Possibly, but you would need a babysitter for the type of meal I'm thinking of."

"That can be easily arranged," Sir assured him.

"Say the word, and I'll get started."

Brie was curious about what Master Anderson was up to as she walked over to Rytsar's house with Hope. Having warned him that she was coming, he was already at the door to greet them when she arrived.

"You're timing is perfect," he said, grinning at Hope. "I have a special surprise for *moye solntse*."

As she stepped inside, Brie thanked him for watching her.

"As her *dyadya,* it is my duty and privilege to spoil her whenever I'm given the chance." His smile broadened as he took Hope from her. "Come, let me amaze you both."

Rytsar walked them to Hope's room where he pointed to a silver box lying in Hope's crib.

Telling Brie to get it, he sat down cross-legged on the floor with Hope and gestured for Brie to join him. She picked up the pretty box and knelt beside him, looking at it with interest.

"I had this specially made for you," he told Hope, nuzzling noses with her.

"Please do the honors, *radost moya*."

Brie lifted the lid and saw tons of sparkly tissue paper. She threw them in the air and let them float down around them to the sound of Hope's delighted giggles.

She giggled herself when she saw the Matryoshka doll intricately painted in the image of a sexy Rytsar, his palm open showing off his tattoo of the sun. Brie picked it up, turning it over in her hands to admire the remarkable detail. "It's exquisite…"

"I do look good, don't I?" he smirked.

Brie held it out to her little girl. "Look, Hope, it's your *dyadya*."

Hope reached out to touch it, her dimples showing

as she smiled.

Brie opened the wooden doll to reveal a figure of Sir dressed in the suit he wore at their wedding. "Oh, your daddy looks so handsome, doesn't he?" she asked Hope.

Examining it, Brie was touched by all the small details, including the spray of bougainvillea in his lapel.

Opening it up, Brie squeaked when she found a replica of herself wearing her lace wedding dress. "This is so beautiful."

"Yes, you are," Rytsar stated. He took it from her to show Hope. "Your mama is the most beautiful woman on this Earth."

Brie blushed when he handed it back to her. "These are amazing."

His blue eyes sparkled with delight. "Go on. There are more."

She opened the doll and giggled. "Oh, my goodness, it's my dad!" The artist had done a phenomenal job capturing his serious expression.

"There's your grandpa," she said, showing Hope. "Don't let his serious expression fool you, little girl. He's a big softie when it comes to you."

It came as no surprise when the next doll turned out to be her mother. The sweet expression painted on her face was charming. The artist was so skillful that he'd been able to capture the similar facial characteristics she shared with her mother.

Brie was super curious about who was next. When she opened it, tears came to her eyes seeing Alonzo holding his beloved violin.

"This is...so touching," she choked out.

Rytsar nodded. "He is a part of her life."

Brie pointed out the violin to Hope. "That's your Grandpa Alonzo's violin. He was a master at playing it." Her heart melted when Hope reached out to touch it with her tiny fingers.

Shaking the doll, Brie realized there were still more. "How many are in here?" she asked Rytsar in amazement.

He only smiled.

Curious about who was next, Brie opened it and burst out in a smile. "Nonno!"

Like with her own mother, the artist had captured the similarities between Sir, Alonzo, and Sir's grandfather. Brie cuddled the doll against her chest, totally in love with the likeness.

She opened the next one and was thrilled to see Nonna's twinkling eyes and warm smile. Brie had never forgotten how kind the old woman had been to her when they first met in Italy. Nonna had made Brie feel like family starting that very first day.

Brie shook the doll and realized there was one more left. She gave it to Hope to shake, too, before she opened it.

Instead of shaking it, Hope handed it to Rytsar.

When he tried to give it to Brie, she wouldn't take it. "Nope, Hope wants you to open it."

Rytsar smirked as he opened the last one and held it up for them to see.

Brie squealed in delight. "Shadow!"

It seemed completely fitting that the very last doll was Hope's guardian angel in cat form.

Rytsar set each doll down in a circle around Hope. "See? *Moye solntse* is surrounded by love."

Brie shook her head, profoundly touched by seeing his words laid out in physical form. She understood that this was his way of remaining a part of Hope's life even when they were thousands of miles apart.

"Rytsar, this is the most beautiful gift that has ever been made."

He winked at her.

Rytsar set Hope on his lap and pointed to his doll. "Notice that your *dyadya* is the biggest of all."

Her heart full, Brie returned to their house with a huge smile on her face.

She was surprised to see that Master Anderson and Sir had already begun preparations for the meal.

"What can I do to help?" she asked.

"Prepare thyself, woman," Master Anderson answered.

Sir looked up and smiled. "You are having a lesson in objectification."

Thrilled beyond words, Brie headed to the bedroom to shower. She was meticulous as she prepared her body. No scented soaps touched her skin as she washed and shaved her body bare.

Toweling off, Brie looked in the mirror as she applied minimal makeup to accentuate her eyes and lips. She put her hair up in a pretty bun with a few loose curls to frame her face.

Certain she had the look of a classy serving platter, she walked out of the bedroom completely naked and headed to the kitchen. Master Anderson put his knife down, letting out an appreciative whistle.

Sir's captivating smile left Brie breathless. "You look stunning, babygirl."

She bowed gracefully. "Thank you, Sir. Where would you like me?"

Master Anderson looked at Sir. "May I do the honors?"

"Of course. You are the guest."

Walking over to Brie, Master Anderson swept her off her feet and laid her down on the cold marble on the center island, which perfectly framed her body. Brie finally realized why Sir insisted on having the size of the island reproportioned during the renovations. He'd had this very purpose in mind.

"You make an alluring display for lunch, darlin'," Master Anderson complemented.

Sir walked over, running his hand over the length of her body, causing pleasant goosebumps on her skin. "A fine display, indeed."

Brie turned her focus on the ceiling as she had been taught at the Training Center, but Sir cupped her chin and turned her head to meet his gaze. "For this scene, you may interact with us."

A smile spread across her face. "Thank you, Sir."

It was silly fun to lie there, watching them slice the ingredients, carefully layering and rolling the sushi before slicing them into bite-sized pieces and artfully arranging them on her body.

She *loved* that part, watching as they decided where to put the next piece, then the ticklish sensation as they placed it on her skin with chopsticks.

Brie lay still as they covered her, shocked by the sheer amount of sushi they were making, and finally asked, "Why so much?"

Master Anderson's low chuckle rang through the kitchen. "Because your Master and I are starving, young Brie."

"Feel free to cover me from head to toe, then," she offered with a grin.

Sir approached her with another sushi roll. He picked up a piece with his set of chopsticks and placed it strategically on her mound. She found it incredibly erotic, which caused tingles of desire. He picked up the next piece, but instead of placing it near her pussy, he held it in front of her lips.

"Open."

Brie opened her mouth, taking the sushi he offered.

Even that was amazingly sensual and she moaned with pleasure.

"I enjoy watching you eat, babygirl."

Brie felt incredibly spoiled.

The two men continued to lay out the food while sporadically feeding her in the process.

Once her body was covered, Master Anderson grabbed Brie's phone off the counter. "Say sushi!"

Brie laughed as he took the picture.

"Before we partake, let me get a real camera." Sir left the room and returned a short time later with his camera.

He took a series of photos. Lowering the camera when he was finished, Sir winked at her.

God, how she loved the way Sir worshipped her body. He never tired of looking at it and continually came up with creative ways to admire it.

Master Anderson clapped Sir on the shoulder. "I think we have outdone ourselves, buddy. Truly a work of art. Now, let's eat!"

The uncovering was just as sensual as the covering. Both men tickled her skin with the light touch of the chopsticks as they deftly took each piece off her body.

Ever the gentlemen, for every morsel they took for themselves, they each shared one with her, which meant she was eating twice as much as they were. It didn't take long before she had to cry uncle.

"No more please," she giggled.

Master Anderson looked at Sir. "It appears she is filled to the gills."

Sir chuckled as he took a piece from her left nipple and placed it in his mouth, chewing slowly as he stared at her.

Brie's heart began to race. It was extremely sensual watching him eat the food from her body.

She lay quietly, soaking in the experience as she watched both men fill up on sushi and chat with one another.

Brie couldn't imagine a better way to spend an afternoon.

Luckiest girl in the world!

Disconnect

When Brie saw the moving van pull up to Rytsar's house, her heart dropped. She looked over at Sir and whimpered.

"It's happening…"

They walked to his house, surprised that he hadn't told them he was moving out of the house permanently. Staring at the moving van, Brie felt her heart catch. She didn't want this to be their reality.

Maxim answered the door and immediately let them in. "He is in the back bedroom."

Hope's room…

She didn't know how she could possibly let him go.

Rytsar was personally packing Hope's things. When they entered the bedroom, he looked up with a somber expression.

"What's going on?" Sir asked.

He sighed in resignation. "I woke up last night and *knew* it was time."

"But why are you packing all your things?" Brie

asked.

Rytsar looked at her and frowned sadly. "I know myself, *radost moya*. If I have this place to escape to, I will never commit to the boy."

"Will we ever see you again?" she choked out.

He reached for her and enfolded her in his embrace. "Of course. I will come to visit…in time, and I trust you will visit us in Russia."

Brie was crushed by the news.

"What are your plans, then?" Sir asked in an even voice.

"I don't know at this point, but my continued absence only hurts the boy and it is starting to weigh on me."

Sir nodded. "Does this mean you are ready to take on the father role?"

"No, *moy droog*, but I am willing. That will have to be enough."

When Sir frowned at his answer, Rytsar asked, "What is wrong, comrade?"

"I want to fully support you, but I can't shake the feeling that something's off. Do you mind letting me see those paternity tests?"

"Why?" Rytsar snarled. "The results were conclusive and there is no chance they all were tampered with. I made certain of it after what happened to you with Lilly."

"Look, I don't doubt the validity of the tests, but I would like to look them over for my own peace of mind."

"Why do I get the impression that you are lying to

me?" Rytsar growled.

Sir stared at him in disbelief, looking deeply offended. "I would never lie to you."

Rytsar let out a ragged sigh, rubbing his head in frustration. "After learning that I am the father of a boy I never knew existed, it's become hard for me to trust anyone."

In answer, Sir commanded that Brie bare the scar on her wrist, as he rolled up his sleeve to expose his scar. Looking at Rytsar, he stated, "You *never* have to doubt our intentions toward you."

Tears flooded the Russian's eyes. "I know this...forgive me."

Sir put his hand on Rytsar's shoulder. "You will never want for trust or support from us."

Rytsar grunted in understanding, wrapping his arms around them both.

Because he had kept up an appearance of composure when confronted with this unusual twist of fate, Brie had failed to grasp how deep his foundation had been shaken.

Sir left Rytsar's house to pore over the paternity tests. When Brie went to check on him, Sir informed her that he would be leaving and wasn't sure when he would be back.

"What's wrong, Sir?"

"I am taking Gray's advice and making sure I understand the whole picture."

When Sir returned hours later, he was adamant that they speak to Rytsar immediately.

"What did you discover?" she asked, now worried.

"There's no time to explain."

Brie quickly grabbed Hope and followed him outside.

Pounding on the door of Rytsar's home, Sir waited several minutes before Maxim answered it. The inside of the beach house was pure chaos and poor Little Sparrow was running around the house, looking lost and afraid.

Rytsar was oblivious, directing his men, who were assisting the movers as they packed boxes and readied the furniture for the long trip back to Russia.

Brie's heart skipped a beat on seeing the house in such disarray. It made the reality of this move more real to her. She looked to Sir, praying he had good news.

"What's up, comrade?" Rytsar shouted above the din.

"We need to talk—privately."

Rytsar furrowed his brow. "What…now?"

Sir gave him a look, then gestured to the door.

Letting out a frustrated sigh, Rytsar told his men to continue under Maxim's direction.

Following behind Brie, Rytsar placed his hand on her back as he looked down at Hope tenderly.

I will miss this… Brie thought.

Without speaking, Sir walked to the beach and headed toward the water's edge, but Rytsar reached out and stopped him.

"Enough with the mystery. What is this about?"

"Anton, I believe you are being deceived."

Rytsar's eyes narrowed. "Why would you say that?"

Sir glanced at Brie briefly before looking Rytsar in the eyes. "There is reason to question whether the child is yours or not."

Rytsar's nostrils flared in anger. "Don't do this to me! Don't make me question this more than I already have."

Pulling the tests from his suit jacket, Sir opened them, pointing to the results of each one. "These seem conclusive on their own, yes. But, I assume you did not have your brothers tested?"

"Why would I do that?" Rytsar shouted, looking at Sir as if he'd gone mad.

Sir was unaffected by his burst of anger and continued, "It's possible one of them is a better match. Because the five of you have such similar genetics, it's unreasonable to assume paternity based on your blood alone. Getting them all tested would prove conclusively whether or not you are the father."

Brie could see the veins in Rytsar's neck pulsing in rage. "Are you telling me that one of my brothers is trying to pass his bastard child off as mine?"

Sir shook his head. "I make no such claim. However, without a blood sample from all four, you will never know if this child is truly yours."

Brie's heart began to race. She wondered if it were possible.

Rytsar growled ominously. "I hope you are wrong, *moy droog*, because I cannot face another betrayal from my family. I cannot!"

Sir met his rage head on. "There is no point in speculating. Get the tests done so you can face the future with confidence."

"Why did you have to bring this into question now?" he asked resentfully.

Sir put an arm around him. "I have felt unsettled about this whole situation, but it took looking at these tests to help clarify the root of my suspicions. I've spoken to several experts who agree that paternity testing between brothers is inconclusive without a comparison of the results. I know this is difficult for you but, as your brother, it's my duty to make certain no stone is left unturned."

Rytsar growled under his breath. "I cannot deal with the consequences if you are right."

Brie clutched Hope against her and reached out to comfort him with her other hand. "We stand beside you no matter what the future holds, Rytsar."

When Rytsar turned to meet her gaze, the torment she saw in those sad blue eyes just about did her in. He'd lost too much, been hurt by too many, to face the possibility of this kind of betrayal.

Looking up to the heavens, he cried, "Tatianna and *Mamulya*, you know I accepted my fate. I *cannot* go back to questioning everything again."

Brie and Sir stood beside him in silent solidarity.

When Hope began to fuss, Rytsar glanced down at her and immediately ripped off his shirt.

"Your skin is burning, *moye solntse*," he said in concern as he shielded her from the rays of the sun with his shirt.

Rytsar's love for Hope was unquestionable. Because of that, Brie had been surprised when he'd mentioned not feeling an immediate attachment to the boy when they first met. At the time, she had discounted it, chalking it up to the shock of the situation.

Now, Brie wondered if Rytsar had instinctually picked up on the fact that the child was one of his brothers and not his.

If the boy isn't his…Rytsar will have no reason to move.

It was a selfish thought and Brie quickly pushed it away. She understood the terrible betrayal Rytsar would face if the boy turned out not to be his. He didn't deserve to suffer that level of treachery.

"I'm unsure I want to know, comrade," Rytsar confessed to Sir.

"You couldn't live without knowing any more than I could."

"But, I may not survive the consequences of the truth."

"You will, because we won't let you fall."

Rytsar halted the move temporarily and then wasted no time in hiring a medical team to visit each brother to perform a full physical "for insurance purposes."

Knowing that the results might prove devastating for Rytsar, Sir pushed back his schedule for the week and arranged a babysitter for Hope so they could travel with him to Russia. He felt it was important that they both be there when Rytsar got the results.

As Brie and Sir packed for the trip, she admitted, "I'm feeling conflicted."

"How so, babygirl?"

"If this child is Rytsar's, we lose him, but I know he will be a good father. If it turns out the child is not his, I'm afraid it will break Rytsar in a way he hasn't experienced before."

Sir wrapped his arms around her. "That is why we must stand strong for him. Whichever way this plays out, Rytsar is going to lose something."

It broke Brie's heart. "It's not fair, Sir."

"Nothing about this situation is fair to him."

During their conversation, Hope had belly-crawled over to Sir and grabbed his pants leg. He leaned down and swept her up into the air.

"Come to Papa!"

Brie smiled as she watched Sir with Hope. For a man who had been afraid of the kind of father he would be, Sir had grown into the role as naturally as breathing. It had taken no effort on his part, despite his many fears.

She knew Rytsar would be the same. In fact, she was certain of it—as long as he was given the chance.

Brie was suddenly struck by a brilliant idea. "Sir, if Rytsar does end up moving, would you consider buying a place in Russia as a second home?"

Sir chuckled. "Funny you should mention that."

Taking Hope with him, he headed into his office and then came out carrying a manila folder. Grinning, he handed it to her. "Great minds think alike."

Brie opened it and started laughing as she scanned

through the papers. "There has to be at least fifteen different homes here."

"I was curious about what was available in Moscow. It would be a financial burden, but we can make the adjustments necessary to accommodate it."

"Anything worth doing requires sacrifice," Brie agreed. She sat down at the kitchen table and spread them all out, her heart quickening as she looked at the houses in Rytsar's homeland.

Sir leaned down and kissed Brie on the top of her head. "Check those over while I take our little princess for a diaper change."

While she waited for them to return, Brie picked out three houses that had caught her eye. For Brie, however, the deciding factor would be the distance from Rytsar's residence.

Although he had completely restored his family mansion after the fire, she knew he rarely visited it.

He'd recently confessed to her, "After losing the last of my mother's personal belongings in the explosion and the fire that followed, I've never felt a desire to go back there."

"Even though it's part of the Durov heritage?"

He smiled sadly. "While I'm certainly a Durov descendant, the only blood I identify with is my mother's—and there was nothing left of her things after the fire."

Brie felt his pain. It must have been unbearable to lose not only his mother but every single physical reminder of her as well.

"Who lives there now?" she'd asked.

"No one. I invite people who have been loyal to the

Durov family to stay whenever they visit Moscow. I see no reason to let it sit idle."

"So, no one lives there permanently?"

It disturbed Brie for some reason, even though it was Rytsar's to do with as he saw fit. But, she'd felt compelled to ask, "How do your brothers feel about that?"

He looked at her and shrugged. "I do not know, *radost moya*. They never bothered to tell me."

Despite the dicey reconciliation he'd had with Andrev after the rescue, Brie was aware that they had not gathered as a family since. Each of the brothers had gone back to living his own life apart from the others.

It seemed his father's plan to break them apart was still playing out long after his death. How sad to think that not even Rytsar's near-death experience had been enough to bring the five brothers back together.

Now, Rytsar was facing the possibility that one of his brothers had gotten Sasha pregnant and was trying to make him believe it was his.

With such an immense fortune at stake, Brie knew there was no limit to what people were capable of.

When Sir returned with Hope, Brie pointed to all the houses she'd picked out and asked, "Are there any here that caught your eye, Sir?"

He leaned in to give her a kiss. "The only requirement I have for any home is that you are in it."

Brie laughed softly as she took his face in her hands and returned his kiss with a deeper one. "Just when I think I can't love you anymore, Sir, you go and say something like that…"

Clash

Three days later, Rytsar, Sir and Brie were waiting in a large doctor's office in downtown Moscow. The doctor was five minutes late and Brie was struggling to stay still, jittery as she was about the results.

She could feel waves of anxiety rolling off Rytsar as he paced back and forth. Sir chose to stand beside Brie, but he eyed his friend with concern.

Unfortunately, nothing anyone could say at this point would comfort him. At least Rytsar would soon know the truth.

Brie and Sir moved to stand beside Rytsar when the doctor walked in.

He held out his hand to Rytsar and shook it firmly. "I'm Doctor Orlov. Please take a seat, Mr. Durov."

"*Nyet.*"

When Rytsar refused, he looked to Brie and Sir. "Please sit."

The doctor sighed when no one made use of the chairs. Walking over to his desk, he sat down and looked up at the three of them. Adjusting his glasses, he placed five files on the desk.

"My team has been very thorough, as I understand the importance of the results here."

"Good," Rytsar stated.

"I had the blood samples sent to several different facilities around the world to compare the results."

"And…?" Rytsar prodded.

Without answering, he opened each file and turned it around so Rytsar could read the results himself. "In every case, despite the similarities of the genetics between you as brothers, each facility came up with the same result."

Rytsar folded his arms, preparing himself for the answer. "Tell me, then. Who is the boy's father?"

Doctor Orlov swallowed hard before answering. "Vlad Durov is clearly the father of this child."

Rytsar said nothing but he reached out to the chair closest to him and slowly sat down.

"Vlad…" His voice was full of shock and disappointment.

Brie sat down in the chair next to him and lightly placed her hand on his thigh, offering her support.

Sir stood beside Rytsar, the picture of masculine protection, but neither of them could do anything to prevent the pain he was experiencing as he absorbed the news.

"The boy is not mine," he stated in a tortured voice.

Brie closed her eyes, swallowing the lump in her throat.

Rytsar had accepted he had a son and was ready to change his life, move back to Russia, and create a family for the little boy by partnering with Sasha.

Now... Everything had changed.

Not only was he not a father, but Sasha had clearly lied to him. What made the deception even more unbearable was that he now knew his oldest brother had fathered the child and had kept it a secret for two years—until now.

Rytsar sat in stunned silence, a look of devastation on his face.

"There is no chance of an error?" Sir asked the doctor.

"It was conclusive for all five facilities."

Pulling a flask from his breast pocket, Sir told Rytsar, "You look like you could use this."

Rytsar took it from him and swallowed a long draught of the vodka. Afterward, he wiped his mouth and held the flask up to Sir.

"No need to share." Sir reached into his other breast pocket and pulled out a second flask. "I've brought my own."

Rytsar snorted, then tipped the flask back, taking another long draught.

Brie sat there with him, wishing desperately she could do or say something to help him with the shock. After Rytsar finished the flask, he patted her hand, then stood up.

Nodding to the doctor, he gathered the five files from the desk and turned to face his friends.

"We are done here."

"If you have any further questions, please don't hesitate to call," the doctor said, holding out his business card.

Rytsar didn't take it. Instead, he tucked the files under his arm. "You've given me everything I need to know."

Sir and Brie followed Rytsar out of the office, and the three walked back to the car in silence.

Once in the car, Rytsar told one of his men, "Call Vlad and tell him to meet me at the mansion. Stress that time is of the utmost importance and that lives depend on it."

After the driver started heading to the family mansion, Sir asked, "Are you sure you want us to be present?"

"Are you not my brother?"

"I am."

"Then, it is only right that you be there when I confront the maggot."

Brie looked at Sir with concern. The fact that Rytsar had just called Vlad a maggot did not bode well.

"Is there anything I can do?" she asked, hoping to ease his mind.

"*Da*, be a woman I can trust," Rytsar said with a catch in his voice.

Brie glanced at Sir, hurt that Rytsar would ever doubt her. "You can always trust me."

Rytsar looked at Brie and sighed. "My level of trust has been eroded. I apologize for disparaging your honor, *radost moya*. I know you are like my mother in your loyalty."

Brie wrapped her arms around him, touched by the comparison. "It's okay. I know you've been hit in the gut by this news."

He nodded, tears coming to his eyes. "Why lie? That little boy doesn't deserve this."

Brie kissed his cheek gently. "Neither do you."

Rytsar sucked in his breath. "That child has been neglected by his father for two years. I will not let Vlad continue to disown him."

Brie was moved that Rytsar's overriding thought was for the child despite the toll this revelation had taken on him personally.

Sir cautioned him. "At this point, we don't know Vlad's level of involvement."

Rytsar glared at him. "Well, we know that his sperm was involved!"

"Hear me out. If Sasha waited this long to tell you, there's a strong possibility Vlad was kept in the dark as well."

Rytsar snarled. "I suppose that might explain why I wasn't approached sooner if both of them are gunning for my inheritance."

"It might," Sir agreed. "I'm certain there is more to this deception than we know."

"Still…Vlad is a married man with children of his own. He should be taking care of his own household, not making bastard children with one of my subs."

"While I agree his morals are lacking, we should not automatically assume he was involved in the deception."

Brie knew it would be less of a blow for Rytsar if Vlad were unaware of the child. However, it would thrust Vlad into the same position that Rytsar had been in. As upsetting as it was for the men, Brie knew the child would suffer the most and she felt sorry for him.

Rytsar nodded in response to Sir, but he looked less than convinced. "As for Sasha…she will regret this in ways she can't imagine."

Once they arrived at the mansion, Rytsar directed them to the gallery room, saying, "The historical society created replicas of as many paintings as they could after the fire."

Brie walked around the large room lined with paintings of the Durov family dating back four hundred years. There was no mistaking Rytsar was part of their family because so many of the men shared his features.

She noticed a picture of a woman set apart from the others on the farthest wall and walked up to it. Rytsar stood next to her as she studied it. Brie was drawn to the woman's kind smile and soulful eyes. "Is that your mother?"

Rytsar nodded. "I had the painter create it based on my memory of her. It is a good likeness."

"She's beautiful."

"Yes, she was."

Brie noted that there was no painting of his father on the wall, and she found that oddly comforting. The man did not deserve to be remembered.

Rytsar turned to Sir. "I think it's the perfect place to confront Vlad, don't you?" He added with an angry laugh, "This way he can make his confession in front of the entire family."

Maxim walked into the room and announced, "Vlad has arrived."

"Send him to me."

Rytsar directed them to stand beside him. He clenched his jaw as he stared at the door, waiting.

While the doctor had spoken in English at Rytsar's request during the office appointment, Brie knew that would not be the case with his brother. Based on what Rytsar had shared, Vlad had no use for foreigners or the English language."

"Do not worry, *radost moya*. My brother does not use big words. You should have no problem understanding what he says."

As soon as Vlad entered the room, Brie was struck by how much he looked like Rytsar.

When Vlad saw Sir, he scowled. "What is the meaning of this, Anton? You claimed it was a matter of life or death."

"I said lives depended on it," Rytsar corrected him coldly.

Vlad eyed Sir suspiciously while completely ignoring Brie.

Brie stared openly at him, unable to get over how much Vlad looked like Rytsar. It was like looking at an older version of Rytsar, except that Vlad had a head of hair and he did *not* have kind eyes.

Rytsar jumped right in. "I know you cheated on your wife with Sasha."

His brother's eyes widened, but he quickly hid his surprise with a dark scowl. "I have no idea what you're talking about."

"There is no point in denying it. I have evidence," Rytsar snarled.

Vlad's heated gaze returned to Sir and he growled at Rytsar, "I don't appreciate having an audience."

Rytsar sneered. "You should have thought of that before you fucked her."

Pointing at Sir, Vlad demanded, "Is he the one feeding you these lies?"

"My brother does not lie."

Vlad's nostrils flared. "I *hate* that you call him that."

Rytsar smiled. "Would you like to know who told me?"

"Yes!"

"Sasha."

Vlad's jaw dropped. "Why the hell would she tell you?"

Rytsar snorted, glaring angrily. "Why do you think?"

Vlad frowned. "It's irrelevant. That was years ago."

"Two, to be exact," he answered, studying his brother's face.

Vlad's frown deepened. "Why would she go to you now? It makes no sense."

Brie glanced at Sir and noticed he was quietly observing Vlad during their exchange. She suspected he was assessing Vlad's tone of voice, body language, and facial expression.

But Brie's full attention was on Rytsar. She didn't want to see him hurt and would do anything to protect him.

The silence in the room stretched on as Rytsar and

Vlad stared each other down.

"It was a short affair. Doesn't even count," Vlad finally grumbled dismissively.

Rytsar took in a slow, deep breath, and glanced at Sir. "I'm struggling not to hit him, comrade."

Sir nodded in understanding.

Rytsar refocused his attention on Vlad. "When was the last time you spoke with Sasha?"

"We haven't spoken since…" He closed his eyes, muttering under his breath, "It ended badly."

Rytsar narrowed his eyes. "Why? What did you do to her?"

Vlad opened his eyes and took a threatening step toward Sir. "This is not for a foreigner's ears, much less a *woman's*." His tone was dismissive as he stared directly at Brie.

"This woman is worth a thousand of you!" Rytsar shouted.

Vlad huffed, spitting on the floor next to Brie.

In the blink of an eye, Rytsar had his hand wrapped around his brother's throat. "You will apologize to her this instant or I will make your wife a widow."

Vlad's face grew bright red as he struggled unsuccessfully to escape his brother's deadly grasp. When his eyes began to bulge, he finally nodded.

The instant Rytsar let go, Vlad grabbed at his throat, coughing violently. Once he could breathe again, he glanced at Brie and croaked out an apology.

Brie inclined her head in acknowledgment, refusing to talk to the man.

"You will treat Mrs. Davis with the same respect you

showed our mother."

Vlad's gaze darted to Brie and then back to Rytsar. He opened his mouth but then quickly shut it again, choosing to say nothing.

"Why do you think Sasha contacted me, Vlad?" Rytsar asked, his voice dripping with contempt.

"Blackmail."

Rytsar's eyes narrowed.

Vlad chuckled with spite. "But, why would she try to blackmail me now?" His left eye twitched. "Why would she be that cruel?"

"Cruel?" Rytsar prodded, wanting to hear more.

Vlad shifted on his feet, giving Sir and Brie a distrustful glance. "Sasha knew how I felt and what I was willing to give up for her. What a heartless bitch."

Rytsar folded his arms and demanded, "Why did it end between you?"

"I told you. She's a heartless cunt."

"Are you saying she broke it off, not you?"

Vlad frowned. "Why? What did she tell you?"

When Rytsar didn't immediately respond, he took a step closer, getting in Rytsar's face. *"What did she tell you?"*

Rytsar was not straightforward in his answer. "She wanted to reconnect with me."

Vlad swallowed hard, stepping back. "With you? But, why?"

Rytsar said nothing.

Vlad gave Rytsar a thumbs up. Brie knew the gesture meant "asshole".

"You want to gloat, Anton? Is that what this is about?" Turning away from him, Vlad stormed out.

"Do not leave!" Rytsar commanded.

Vlad turned around. Brie could see the veins in his neck pulsing with rage. "There is nothing you can say to keep me here, Anton."

"Sasha has a child."

Vlad's jaw fell and he stood frozen in place. "How old?"

"Two."

Vlad's lips formed a thin line as he digested the news. "Yours?" he finally asked.

Rytsar shook his head.

Vlad stared at him, licking his lips nervously.

"You didn't know?" Rytsar asked in a sarcastic tone.

Brie cried out when Vlad suddenly rushed Rytsar, cocking his fist back to punch him in the face. Quick as lightning, Sir had Vlad's arm behind his back, immobilizing the man before he even knew what had happened.

"Liar!" Vlad tried unsuccessfully to break Sir's hold. "You fucking liar!" he screamed again, becoming so upset that spittle escaped his mouth.

Brie was surprised by how violently he was struggling against Sir. He was acting like a madman, but Sir's grip was tight and he could not escape.

"I would never lie about a child," Rytsar growled.

Eventually, Vlad stopped struggling against Sir and became still. In time, the room filled with the sound of his labored breathing as he took in the news.

Vlad looked at Rytsar. "If the child isn't yours, then…"

"Yes, the boy is yours."

Vlad turned his head away.

Brie watched as Rytsar's angry glare transformed into a look of compassion for his brother.

Sir released Vlad, but he didn't move.

Instead, he turned back to Rytsar and asked, "Anton, why did she keep it a secret from me?"

"I don't know. Sasha told me that the boy was mine."

"What?" Vlad yelled. Pounding his chest several times, he demanded, "Why would she do that when the child is *mine*?"

Rytsar didn't answer.

Brie watched as understanding slowly crept into Vlad's eyes. Soon, he snarled in disgust, "She's after the money…"

"That fucking inheritance," Rytsar answered with equal venom.

Vlad looked at Rytsar, slowly shaking his head in disbelief. "I have a son."

"Yes, another son, on top of the three you've already fathered with your wife," Rytsar said with disgust.

Vlad's eyes flashed with anger. "Sasha was mine before I ever met Zoya, and long before you started fucking her."

"What are you talking about?"

"Father didn't consider Sasha a good match for our family, but I defied him by continuing to see her behind his back. So, he did the one thing he knew that would rip my heart out." Vlad spat on the floor. "He took her away from me and served her up to you so you could play with her in your dungeon."

Rytsar looked at him in shock. "I never knew this."

"You didn't even care about her, treating her like a slut, when I loved her. She was *mine*, Anton!"

"Father used Sasha to punish you. I had nothing to do with it."

"But you were the one who fucked her!"

"I swear to you I would never have touched her, had I known."

"It doesn't matter. You see, I learned my lesson and played the dutiful son, marrying a woman I didn't love to further our family's influence." He laughed sarcastically. "And, I did it for nothing because *you* received the inheritance."

The rumbling growl from deep in Rytsar's chest was low and ominous. "I thought I could not despise our father any more than I do, but this proves how truly evil he was."

Vlad shook his head. "And now, I find out I fathered a child with the woman I loved, and she didn't even tell me."

Rytsar slapped him on the back. "We will confront her tomorrow so we can get answers, but you must do one thing first."

He narrowed his eyes. "What?"

"You must admit your betrayal to your wife. If we eliminate her ability to blackmail us, she will be at our mercy."

"I won't do it," he declared stubbornly.

"You must, or Sasha will make certain Zoya hears it from someone else."

Brie could see Vlad's defenses going up.

He looked suspiciously at Rytsar. "How do I even

know the child is mine? Am I just supposed to take your word for it?"

"He had all four of you tested under my recommendation," Sir informed him.

Vlad glared at Sir, then turned on Rytsar. "You had us tested without our consent?"

"Of course," Rytsar answered smoothly. "How else was I to discover which of my brothers was sleeping with Sasha behind his wife's back?"

"Well, now you know why," he answered harshly.

"So, you'll tell Zoya?" Rytsar asked.

Vlad looked as if he was about to punch Rytsar again.

Sir defused the situation by stating, "At this point, we do not know Sasha's intentions. Taking away her ability to blackmail you may help ensure the boy's safety."

As soon as Sir mentioned the boy, Brie saw Vlad's entire countenance change. "I will think on it."

"Make atonement to your wife," Rytsar advised him.

Vlad's hackles went back up. "Don't tell me how to handle my life, Anton. No one gets to control me anymore—least of all you!"

He turned abruptly and walked out.

Rytsar called after him, "Make *Mamulya* proud."

Vlad clenched his fists but continued walking without saying another word.

"You do like to provoke him," Sir observed after he was gone.

"It's payback. He was the worst of my brothers growing up, purposely getting himself in trouble just to see me beaten at the whipping pole."

"After today's revelation, it's clear your father was strategic in using you against them to ensure their obedience to him."

Rytsar sneered. "I wish I could raise him from the dead just so I could torture him for all the wrongs he has committed against me and my family."

Reaching out to Brie, Rytsar pulled her close. She was grateful he had survived the confrontation with Vlad.

As Brie laid her head against Rytsar's chest, she gazed over at Sir, wondering what tomorrow would bring.

Twisted Fate

When Vlad arrived at the mansion the next day, he had dark circles under his bloodshot eyes.

Rytsar seemed amused by it. "So, you told your wife, then?"

Vlad growled in answer.

"How did it go?"

"I slept with the dogs."

Rytsar's lips twitched. "Good. Then you are ready for this meeting."

Vlad frowned. "No, Anton, I am not. But I want to see my son."

Brie hadn't cared for Vlad up to this point. So, it surprised her that she suddenly felt a spark of compassion for the man. It seemed Vlad genuinely cared about the child.

At the appointed time, the four of them left to confront Sasha. Brie was grateful that Rytsar had insisted they attend. Sir would prove effective as a mediator, should things become dicey.

When Rytsar pulled up to a hotel, Vlad demanded angrily, "Why are we meeting her here?"

Rytsar shrugged. "It's where we always meet. I didn't want to arouse suspicion."

Vlad snarled, clearly unhappy with the location.

"Will the boy be there?" Sir asked.

"*Da*, I asked that she bring him today."

Looking at Vlad, Rytsar said, "You deserve to see your son."

Vlad nodded curtly.

Brie let out a nervous sigh as they walked into the hotel. This was going to be an ugly confrontation. Sasha had no idea that Vlad would be there or that Rytsar knew he was not the father. There was no way this was going to end well for her.

Rytsar unlocked the door to the room and allowed Brie to enter first. She was impressed by the large suite. It sported a formal living area, dining room, wet bar, and kitchen.

Vlad snorted in disgust, obviously jealous, as he glanced around the spacious suite. Looking at his watch, he told Rytsar, "She should be here any minute."

Rytsar shook his head. "Sasha is notoriously late."

"That's not true," Vlad insisted. "I've never known her once to be late."

Rytsar shrugged. "She likes to be punished."

Vlad's nose crinkled up in disgust. "Damn it, Anton, I don't want to know that."

"It's obvious we know two different sides of the woman."

Vlad ran his fingers through his hair nervously, reminding Brie of Rytsar when he rubbed his head. Apparently, it was a nervous tick they both shared.

Fifteen minutes later, Rytsar's phone pinged and he glanced at the text. "She's here."

Brie's heart skipped a beat, wondering about how this would go.

"I want all of you to stand out of her line of sight so she doesn't notice you until after she's entered the room," Rytsar told them.

When Brie heard the excited chatter of a child running down the hallway, she noticed Rytsar and Vlad tense.

She held her breath when the door swung open and the little boy burst into the room. He toddled up to Rytsar and craned his head up, smiling at him.

Sasha walked in. She laughed as she shut the door. "Just look at how he loves you…" Her smile faded when she saw the other three standing there.

"Viktor, come here," she commanded.

The little boy toddled back to her and she grabbed his hand, pulling him closer.

"Rytsar…what are they doing here?"

"I'm positive you know," Rytsar answered, his voice cold as ice.

She shook her head. "Rytsar, you don't understand."

"But I do. I know Vlad is the father of this boy."

She shot a nervous glance at Vlad.

"Why did you keep him a secret, Sasha?" Vlad demanded.

"I…" She paused a moment, beads of perspiration forming on her forehead. "Vlad, Viktor is the best thing in my life. I didn't tell you because I didn't want to share him with anyone."

"That wasn't your right!" he roared.

The little boy whimpered, grabbing his mother's legs. She winced when she picked him up but wrapped her arms around him protectively. Turning to Vlad, she warned, "Lower your voice. You're scaring him."

Vlad's nostrils flared and he opened his mouth to respond, but Rytsar interrupted. "You lied to us both. We have every right to be angry with you."

"But Viktor isn't to blame," she answered, looking at her son. "He's done nothing wrong."

"Why didn't you tell me about my son?" Vlad demanded.

The little boy started crying and Sasha pressed his head against her chest, murmuring. "Hush…hush…little one."

Rytsar looked at the boy with compassion. "We are not here to scare the boy, but we expect answers."

Sasha gazed up at him. "I never meant for this to happen."

"Explain."

She closed her eyes for a moment, letting out a long sigh. Glancing at Vlad, she told them, "When I had the affair, I was trying to recapture a part of my youth…to experience those feelings of young love again."

Vlad's eyes softened.

She looked at him sadly. "It was selfish, I know." She kissed the top of her son's head. "But I'm not sorry for it, because God gifted me with Viktor. How could I ever regret something so beautiful?"

Rytsar frowned, unmoved by her words. Pointing to Vlad, he said, "You denied your son his father for two years. Then you compounded it by lying to me about who the real father was."

"I know...I never planned this. I was thoroughly happy living on my own with my son. But life isn't always fair."

"Explain."

Sasha looked at Rytsar with sympathy. "It wasn't right to involve you, but I would do anything for my son. Even if it meant deceiving you to get what I want."

Rytsar's eyes narrowed.

Sir addressed her. "What is it you aren't telling them?"

Instead of answering him, Sasha looked to Brie. "You would understand. I know you have a daughter. If you knew you were dying, wouldn't you do everything possible to ensure her future?"

Sasha said the word "dying" so casually that Brie felt time stop for a moment. She couldn't imagine having to face such a thing. It would be too terrible to bear.

"...looking at my options, I knew what I had to do for my boy. Vlad already had a family."

Sasha looked at Rytsar. "What I needed was someone fully devoted to my boy, and that man is you. You are what's best for Viktor."

Vlad pounded his chest, pain infusing his voice, "I love you, Sasha. I've always loved you. Does that mean nothing?"

"I'm sorry, Vlad."

"Sorry?" he cried out. "What makes you think that

means anything in a situation like this? First, you break my heart by telling me you're dying, and then you crush it by telling me you want someone else to raise my son?"

"You were never supposed to know," she said with tears in her eyes. "I didn't want to hurt you."

Vlad looked away from her, struggling to contain his emotions.

"Dying or not, that is not a decision you get to make," Rytsar stated. "Vlad is the boy's biological father."

Vlad faced her again and insisted, "Let me at least hold my boy."

She nodded, letting Vlad take the child from her arms.

Sasha stood back and watched them with a sad, far-off look in her eyes as Vlad held the boy up and smiled at him.

Brie felt sympathy for the woman despite the fact that she had purposely deceived both men.

"Where do we go from here?" Rytsar asked her.

Sasha dabbed at her eyes. "I don't know. I never planned for this day."

"How long do you have, Sasha?" Sir asked her.

She frowned, sighing. "The survival rate is horrifyingly low for pancreatic cancer, and I'm in the advanced stages. Each day it becomes harder and harder to hold my son."

"How can this be? You don't look like you're dying," Vlad protested.

She gave him a sad smile. "It's a silent killer. That's what makes it so deadly. I went in for severe back pain and left knowing I would die within the year." She looked at Rytsar. "The day I got the diagnosis, I wrote you the letter. I knew I didn't have much time."

"You should have told me," Rytsar said with great sorrow.

"I didn't want pity."

Rytsar cupped her chin and gazed deep into her eyes. "I can see you are in pain. I am sorry this is your fate, *lisichka*."

She gave him a tender look on hearing him call her by her pet name.

"I will be okay as long as I know Viktor will be taken care of."

Vlad walked to her with Viktor in his arms. "I pledge my life to this boy."

Sasha nodded, seemingly accepting this twist of fate. "He looks at home in your arms, Vlad."

Smiling, she gave her son several kisses on the cheek.

The mood was somber on the drive back, but Brie took comfort in watching Vlad with the boy. Sasha had insisted that Vlad take Viktor for a few hours so the two could get to know one other. It resulted in Vlad comforting an unhappy child who was missing his mother, but he was patient with Viktor.

"What are you going to do with the boy after she passes?" Rytsar asked.

"Zoya would never turn a child away."

"Even knowing the circumstances?" Rytsar asked.

"She may hate me now, but she has a tender heart for children."

Rytsar nodded. "I will have the lawyers contact you to establish your parental rights."

"Good," Vlad grunted.

Vlad turned to his son, wiping the tears from his cheeks. "I'm here, Viktor. Your father is not going anywhere."

Brie caught Rytsar staring at them. "What are you thinking?"

"That there is not enough vodka in all of Russia to help me cope with the last two days."

Vlad left with his son shortly after they arrived at the mansion but, before he made his way to the door, he told Rytsar, "I still do not like you, Anton. You're an arrogant ass. But, I have to thank you for uniting me with my son. If it hadn't been for you..." He started to choke up and had to start again. "If it hadn't been for you, I would have never known Viktor was my son."

Rytsar looked down, swallowing hard. "And it's because of you that I get the chance to spend time with Sasha before she dies." His voice caught, and he shook his head. "It means more to me than you know."

Vlad lifted his head, looked Rytsar in the eye, and held out his hand. "I forgive you."

"For what?"

"For your involvement with Sasha."

Rytsar stared at his brother's outstretched hand for several moments, contemplating it before taking it and shaking it firmly.

Brie was stunned.

After Vlad left, they went up to him and Sir asked, "Did you really just shake his hand?"

"I was shocked at first, *moy droog*, I won't lie. I never asked for his forgiveness—nor do I want it. But, as I was staring down at his hand, I realized it was something he needed."

He looked at Sir and shrugged. "It's a small thing, but I'm certain my mother would be proud and it cost me nothing to give it."

They returned to the apartment so Rytsar could start on his vodka therapy.

The fourth round in, Rytsar received a phone call and looked to see who it was.

"It's Vlad," he told them, laughing. "He probably wants to shake my other hand."

When Brie saw the expression on Rytsar's face once his brother started talking, she knew the news wasn't good.

Rytsar put down his glass and left them alone in the room.

When he finally returned, he had a dazed look in his eyes.

"What's happened, Rytsar?" Brie asked, her stomach twisting into knots.

He turned to her, unable to speak.

Sir walked over and placed his hand on Rytsar's

shoulder. "What did he say, brother?"

Rytsar looked up at him, distraught. "Sasha jumped off the Krymsky Bridge an hour ago."

"Oh, no…" Brie whimpered.

"Vlad received a text from her just before she jumped."

Rytsar handed over his phone, so they could read it.

"Just when the caterpillar thought the world was ending, it became a butterfly."

Thank you, Vlad.

Now I can fly free.

Tell Viktor I love him.

Loving the Russian

Rytsar, distressed by the news about Sasha, started pacing as soon as they arrived back at the apartment.

Brie and Sir tried to console Rytsar without success.

After watching Rytsar pace back and forth relentlessly for over an hour, Sir took Brie aside. "Our friend is struggling. Too much has happened for him to cope."

"I know, Sir. It's so sad…"

She looked at Rytsar, her heart aching for him.

Sir shared, "Anton once told me that the power in BDSM lies in the fact that it takes the physical and mixes it with the spiritual to create internal balance. Our friend is in desperate need of that right now."

"I agree, Sir. I think it would benefit us all."

Sir gave her an unusual command, instructing her to take off her collar and replace it with a collar from Rytsar's tool chest. Her heart raced, wondering what Sir was planning.

Brie nodded to Sir, indicating she understood her

task. Before leaving, she bowed to him and headed to the bedroom to change.

As she was walking away, she heard Sir ask Rytsar, "Would you like me to pour you a shot, old friend?"

"*Da*, peasant! I do not know what took you so long."

Sir's low chuckle followed her down the hallway. Brie smiled, grateful that the two shared such a relationship. Sir had a way of bringing out a lighter side to Rytsar even during stressful times.

Taking extra care to prepare herself, Brie thoroughly washed her skin before spritzing on a light perfume that not only had a pleasant scent, but also a pleasing taste.

Completely naked, she stared into the mirror. She was suddenly hit by an overpowering sense of love for Rytsar.

Tonight, she hoped to express her love in a way that would help heal his hurting heart.

Brie wandered over to Rytsar's bedroom and opened his tool chest, searching through it until she found a collar and leash. She carefully buckled the leather collar around her neck and attached the leash to the metal ring.

The sound of the click as she attached the leash sent a pleasant shiver down her spine.

With a sense of anticipation and love, she picked up the handle of the leash and headed out of the bedroom.

She could hear the two men talking, the tone of their voices somber and quiet. Brie assumed they were discussing what had happened and wondered if she should interrupt.

When Sir saw her, however, he smiled in approval.

Rytsar turned to face her. When their eyes met, her

heart skipped a beat—the connection made.

She walked up to him with the grace of a feline, bowing low at his feet as she lifted the leash to him with open palms.

He made no move toward her.

She looked up at him questioningly.

Although his gaze held untold passion, there was profound sadness behind those intense eyes, and seeing it stole her breath away.

Brie was determined to ease that sadness with the strength of her love.

She let out a soft moan when Rytsar took the leash from her hands and pulled on the chain. Claiming her offer of submission, he lifted her up to meet his lips.

His low groan spoke to her soul, filling her with a need to satiate his desire.

Her Master came up behind her and caressed her shoulders. Tingles of electricity coursed through her body when she felt his touch.

Grazing his fingers lightly over her skin, he murmured, "You are so innocent and beautiful, téa."

"Hold on to my *kotenok*," Rytsar ordered. "I must get something."

He handed Sir the leash and left the room, returning with a strip of red satin clutched in his hand.

Sir smiled. "I like the way you think."

Rytsar took the leash back from Sir and pulled Brie close. "First, you will reacquaint me with your oral skills."

Brie smiled, looking down at the outline of his cock. "It would be my honor, Rytsar."

He raised an eyebrow. "You will call me Anton tonight."

Her eyes widened. Calling Rytsar by his given name changed the whole dynamic of the encounter.

It was no longer a simple scene because it added an emotionally charged element.

Brie glanced at Sir, needing to see his reaction.

When he nodded, she realized he had discussed it with Rytsar while she was in the bedroom.

"And what do I call you, Master?" she asked Sir.

Those sexy lips curled into a smile. In a chocolaty voice, he answered, "You will call me Thane."

Brie felt the butterflies start.

A scene calling both men by their given names…

Sir continued, "Anton and I will do the same with you, Brie."

Her mouth opened in surprise hearing Sir call her by her first name.

Although the change seemed deceptively simple, it was unchartered territory for the three of them.

Rytsar commanded in a seductive voice, "Turn around, Brie."

The butterflies started again as he took her wrists and began binding them with the satin ribbon. The simple act of binding caused her nipples to contract into tight buds.

She looked at Sir, her breath coming in shallow gasps.

"I like seeing you like this," he said huskily.

She bit her lip and smiled.

Rytsar gazed at her with a mixture of tenderness and lust as he pushed her down. "On your knees. You will suck Thane first."

Brie's heart did a flip-flop as Rytsar helped her to the floor with her wrists secured firmly behind her back.

She loved the intoxicating contrast of being in control while being completely helpless…

As both men undressed in front of her, Brie admired the contrast of their bodies. Sir's toned chest covered in dark hair and Rytsar's muscular one covered in scars.

When Sir stepped closer to her with his hard shaft, she looked up at him. She was immediately reminded of the first time she took his cock into her mouth on stage at the Submissive Training Center.

He'd tied her hands back then, as well, helping her to take his shaft deep into her throat.

Everything about Sir was physically pleasing, from his chiseled face all the way down to those powerful thighs that framed his handsome cock.

"Open yourself to me," he commanded in a low, sultry voice.

Brie smiled as she opened her lips to take his shaft into her mouth. After years under his personal instruction, she knew exactly what Sir preferred, which made the satin ribbon restraint unnecessary. However, the memories it evoked of being bound this way helped to heighten her arousal as she wrapped her lips around the head of his cock.

She began by flicking her tongue against his frenulum and around the sensitive ridge of the head. Sir gathered her hair with one hand, using it to guide her, gradually forcing his cock deeper down her throat.

Rytsar grunted his approval when she finally took its

entirety.

Brie kept her eyes on Sir, making muffled moans of pleasure as he began thrusting into her mouth. It was incredible to compare that inexperienced girl who was so determined to deep throat his shaft to the woman she was now who actually took profound pleasure in the act.

Rytsar cleared his throat. "Brie…"

Her heart quickened as she disengaged from Sir with a smile on her lips, before turning her attention on Rytsar.

Meeting the blue intensity of his gaze, she took his rigid cock in her mouth and swallowed, taking the head of his shaft down her throat.

"Go slowly," he commanded.

Normally, Rytsar liked it deep and fast, so she pulled away to start again. This time, she concentrated on his balls first, sucking them, then nibbling up the length of his cock before encasing the head of his shaft with her lips.

He let out a groan of satisfaction as she made love to him with her tongue, teeth, and lips.

"What a difference proper instruction makes," he grunted, glancing over at Sir.

Sir looked down at her proudly. "She has exceeded her instruction."

"*Da…*" Rytsar agreed huskily, taking her head in his hands to stop her. "She may be too good at this point."

Brie's heart swelled with pride on hearing his praise. She tickled his frenulum with her tongue and he immediately pulled out of her mouth, giving her a stern look.

"Such a naughty *kotenok*."

Brie suddenly realized how foolish it was to tease a sadist when Rytsar wrapped his hand around the back of her neck while she was still in a kneeling position. With gentle pressure, he forced her head to the floor.

She lay there with her cheek against the cold marble and her ass in the air.

"I almost came against my will," Rytsar complained to Sir.

Sir smirked in response. "Then she needs to be taught a lesson."

Brie quivered on the floor, knowing she'd been too cocky with her tongue, but deciding it was worth it to know she still had that kind of power over the Russian.

Chills of excitement began to course through her when Rytsar pulled on her leash, helping her to her feet so he could lead her to his bedroom.

After untying the red satin, Rytsar ordered her on the bed and the two men descended on her. Their last encounter in California had been rough and demanding, but tonight they were gentle with her, their caresses light and teasing.

Brie closed her eyes, giving in to their passionate exploration. Sir concentrated on her breasts while Rytsar stroked her pussy with his fingers.

She wanted to join in their exploration, and asked, "May I touch you both?"

Sir looked up from her breast and smiled seductively. "You may, Brie."

Again, she felt a thrill on hearing him speak her given name during the scene.

His sensual lips returned to her, moving from her

nipple to the valley between her breasts where he left a long, slow trail of kisses down to her stomach. Rytsar added to those sensations with playful nibbles up the length of her thigh—both men teasing her to distraction with their talented mouths.

Rytsar had the leash wrapped around his hand, keeping it taut. That light but constant pull on the collar kept her focused on it, adding to the heady feeling of being dominated.

Brie reached out to touch both men, lovingly caressing Rytsar's tattoo-covered shoulder while the fingers of her other hand danced over the toned muscles of Sir's back.

Rytsar pulled on the leash, saying in his sexy Russian accent, "I am going to eat your pussy, Brianna."

Her heart started racing, having never heard Rytsar call her by her formal given name. She watched with heightened attention as he settled between her legs and gave her wet pussy a long, slow lick. He looked up at her and vowed. "I'm going to eat you until you cry out to God."

Brie held her breath as he gripped her buttocks with both hands and buried his face in her mound.

Rytsar swirled his tongue around her clit, and then zeroed in on her most sensitive point, sucking and licking it. Every time the stimulation became too much, he backed off, and her body would start to relax—until he started up again.

Sir took his time worshipping her breasts, tugging and pulling on one nipple while he sucked and licked the other. Both men knew her body so well that every touch, suck and lick brought her closer to climax.

Brie reached down to run her hand over Rytsar's clean-shaven head just before she threw her head back and moaned in ecstasy.

Rytsar stopped momentary and looked up from between her legs. "I do not give you permission to come."

Her eyes widened, unprepared for that command. He started sucking her clit with a teasing rhythm while Sir moved from her breasts to her mouth.

Brie had to fight off the delicious heat the Russian was creating in her nether regions. Sir's gentle kisses contrasted with the intense stimulation Rytsar was creating, and the combination drove her wild.

She moaned louder, squirming against Rytsar's tongue. She heard his low laughter, just before he made slurping sounds as he took things to another level.

Brie's moans soon turned into short gasps as her thighs began to shake.

When he suddenly stopped and swirled his finger slowly around her swollen clit, she knew she was going to lose it.

"Oh, God…oh, God…oh, God…Anton…" she whimpered, trying to stop the orgasm.

Rytsar chuckled as he took another lick. Lifting his wet chin from her pussy, he growled. "Come, Brianna."

She stopped fighting and gave in to the erotic heat he had created. Meanwhile, Sir pressed his lips firmly against hers. Embracing the fire as she tensed for release, Brie let go, crying into Sir's mouth.

Brie felt like a wet noodle afterward, and lay there in a contented daze.

Rytsar pulled on her leash. "I need more."

Chills of excitement flowed over her skin as the two men repositioned her.

Brie settled down on Sir's cock, grinding her sensitive pussy against him, the juicy wet sound of her excitement filling the room.

Sir looked up at her, his eyes searching the depth of hers. "I'm in love with you, Brie."

She felt chills on hearing those words and their power made her heart race.

In the past, whenever the three of them scened together, they'd never blurred the lines of the power exchange. She was Sir's téa and Rytsar's *radost moya*.

But this…this was intensely intimate on a different level.

Sir pulled her down on him so her chest rested against him. He whispered in her ear, "I know your desires. Even those you are afraid to voice aloud…"

She felt tingles, remembering when he had voiced those words at the cabin.

As if on cue, Rytsar came up behind her, grasping her buttocks as he pressed his cock into her tight ass. She purred as he slipped inside, stretching and opening her body to accommodate them both.

"I want to feel my cock deep inside you, Brianna."

She moaned, pushing against him in order to take the full length of his shaft. "Oh, Anton…"

When both men began alternating their strokes, she screamed in ecstasy.

Brie always marveled at how these two men could play with her so seamlessly. It was as if they were as connected to each other as they were to her. There was never a missed step or an awkward moment whenever they scened as a threesome.

She assumed it was due to the many years they'd known each other, the tragedies they'd suffered together, and the unusual bond that they had made as blood brothers.

It was a privilege to be the center of attention with such extraordinary men.

They were thorough in their claiming, seeking to please her in a myriad of ways before seeking release for themselves. There was no doubt that both Rytsar and Sir found immense enjoyment in her pleasure. They never seemed to tire of their sensual connection with her.

But today was different…

It seemed every touch, every taste, was being savored. She cherished the intensity of their lovemaking, and the tears began to fall.

This was a mix of the most profound love and the most intense pleasure.

Brie cried out, moved in a way she'd never experienced before. Sir met that cry by pressing his lips hard against hers, melding his desire with hers.

Who knew such feelings could fuse together to create a sensation so heartbreakingly delicious?

She came again without any warning.

Both men groaned in response.

In a relationship this close, there was no need to hide their true feelings. It allowed all their emotions to exist together in the same moment—love and loss, pain and pleasure, fear and joy.

All of it came together, propelling Brie upward on a sub high unlike anything she had ever experienced before. Both men came inside her while calling her name.

Afterward, they lay in the bed together, the immensity of the love between them still palpable like the sun on their skin.

"Thank you, *radost moya*," Rytsar said, unfastening the collar around her neck. He leaned down and kissed her sweaty skin where the collar had rested. Then, in typical sadist fashion, he bit down, leaving a bruising mark on her throat.

While he tucked a sweaty lock of stray hair behind her ear, she asked him, "Do you feel loved?"

"I do."

He smiled at her before he lay back down on the bed and stared up at the ceiling.

Silence filled the room as they basked in the warmth of each other's presence.

"Are you planning to stay, brother?" Sir asked, finally breaking the silence.

Rytsar blinked slowly several times, before answering. "*Nyet*, I will go back with you. Viktor does not need me anymore."

Brie could hear the subtle ache in his voice and knew he was mourning the loss of the future he'd thought he'd have here.

She slid her hand into his. "I have an idea."

Brie saw a slight smirk as he continued to stare up at the ceiling. "What?"

"What if we bought a house up here? Something perfect for children and close enough to Viktor that he could come for overnights to visit with his *dyadya*?"

Rytsar turned his head. "What are you saying?"

"Sir and I were thinking of getting a second home here in Moscow."

"You were?" he asked, looking at Sir.

"Naturally. It's important to stay close to family."

Smiling excitedly, she told him, "There's no reason you can't use it whenever you return to your homeland."

"I don't take charity," he scoffed.

Brie giggled. "It's not charity. It's a good use for a home that needs people in it."

He smiled as he looked back up at the ceiling. "I may have to join you on your hunt for a house, *radost moya*. To ensure it meets my standards."

Brie grinned, squeezing his hand.

But Rytsar slowly lost his smile. "I should have known something was not right with Sasha."

"No one could have known," Sir assured him.

"But I remember being surprised when Sasha kept pushing hard to get married, despite the casual BDSM relationship we shared."

"You never told us that," Brie said, sitting up to look at him.

Rytsar shrugged. "I saw no reason to mention it because I was at an impasse. While I didn't want the child to remain a bastard, I'd already sworn myself to Tatianna and will marry no other."

Again, Brie was struck by the fact that Rytsar was a condor.

"I'm glad you did not have to make a choice either

way," Sir told him.

Rytsar sighed. "I can't help feeling I failed her."

"Her fate was sealed, brother. There is nothing you could have done to change the outcome. But, you were able to give Sasha the only thing that mattered to her—peace of mind about her son's future."

"I should be angry at her for her lies and the consequences they would have had on me and my family, but…I understand her reasons and feel no resentment toward her." Rytsar turned to look at Sir. "When I got up this morning, I was ready to rip her apart. Crazy the difference twelve hours can make."

Sir frowned. "I never would have guessed the truth behind her lies."

"And I wouldn't have known it if it hadn't been for you," Rytsar replied.

"Truthfully, I did it for me. The only way I could support the future you had chosen was to eliminate any doubt about the validity of her claim. Unfortunately, I am not a very trusting person."

"Me neither, *moy droog*. That's why we get along so well," he laughed.

Brie gave each of them a kiss. "I cannot wait to get back home and snuggle with Hope."

"Yes, I will have to tell *moye solntse* about her cousin in Russia and the herd of ponies I am going to buy her."

Brie giggled. Then, gazing into his blue eyes, she whispered, "Are you really okay, Anton?"

"I will be." He kissed her on the forehead before getting up as he headed to the bathroom.

He returned a few minutes later, drying off his chest

with a towel. He walked up to Sir, who was still lying on the bed beside Brie. Without any warning, he twisted up the towel and snapped it on Sir's thigh.

"What the hell?" Sir yelled, caught off guard by the sneak attack.

Rytsar smirked. "It's time we plan a date for the isle, *moy droog…*"

Their Voices

After returning from Russia, Brie was driven by a burning desire to finish her second documentary. Sasha's death had reminded her of how fleeting life was and it helped spur her on as she devoted countless hours to complete the film.

Brie believed the only way one could truly live on through the ages was through art—and her art was film.

The moment she finished, Brie ran into Sir's office and cried, "I'm done!"

He stood up with open arms and picked her up, twirling her in the air. "Congratulations, babygirl. I'm so proud of you."

When he set her down, they indulged in a long kiss.

Brie could hear Hope bouncing in her bouncy seat, and went to pick her up. Sir had watched over her for weeks so Brie could concentrate on the film. Lifting Hope up, Brie twirled her just as Sir had.

Brie told her, "Mommy is done, so that means it's time to party Hollywood style."

Brie could hardly contain her excitement as she and Lea prepared the house for the big party. Lea had insisted on coming over to help decorate, while Sir and Rytsar went off to rent a giant screen and projector.

Thankfully, Boa had offered to bring hors d'oeuvres for the special viewing, which Brie was eternally grateful for. With Boa in charge, she was guaranteed killer snacks for the event without the stress of having to prepare them herself. In her current state of chaos, it could have spelled disaster and she would never have been able to live that down with Marquis Gray in attendance.

Brie had envisioned something grand and had rented long red velvet curtains with gold, braided ties. She wanted to transform their great room into a movie theater. To enhance the look, she had also rented red velvet Louis chairs to give the room a more theater-like feel.

"Are you nervous?" Lea asked as she helped Brie hang the curtains.

"Not about the film. I think it's great." Brie blushed. "I guess that sounds really conceited of me."

"Not at all, girlfriend. You should feel that way about anything you create. It's a sign that you're confident in your work."

"What I'm really nervous about is if the people I filmed will like how I treated their individual scenes. I really tried to showcase each person and to highlight the important elements of the scene itself, but there were limitations because each one was filmed in a different setting."

"I think that is what is going to make this film incredible. All that variety is bound to capture people's imagination."

"That or it'll end up looking like a hodgepodge of scenes thrown together with no real substance," Brie fretted.

Lea put an arm around her. "You create art, woman. I totally trust your creative eye and that big heart of yours," she said, pressing her hand against Brie's chest. "It's what makes you stand out from all the rest."

Brie sighed, giving her a half-smile. "Well, if everyone coming tonight feels that way, I'll be golden."

Lea squeezed her tight. "I can't believe it. Tonight, we get to see your labor of love that has been years in the making. This is so exciting!"

"I can't tell you how glad I am that you're a part of it."

"Are you kidding? I consider it an honor, Brie."

Once they had the chairs set out, Brie counted them to make sure she hadn't forgotten anyone. As she pointed to each chair, she called out their names. "So, we'll have Rytsar, Tono, you, Autumn, Marquis, Celestia, Ms. Clark, Master Anderson, Shay, Boa, Mistress Lou, Baron, Captain, Candy, Mary, Faelan and Kylie."

Lea tsked. "Wow, those last three could prove an interesting combination."

"I've talked to all three and they said they're fine with it." Brie shrugged. "I guess we'll see if they were telling the truth tonight."

"Can you imagine watching your boyfriend's ex-girlfriend suck his cock on the big screen? Even *I* don't think I could handle it."

Brie laughed. "Thankfully, Kylie has already seen it. I didn't want her to feel blind-sided by watching it the first time with everyone else."

"What did she say after watching it?"

"She said Mary has good skills."

Lea burst out laughing. "Wow, I gotta hand it to her, Kylie's fucking awesome."

"Yeah, I think so, too. I mean, it'd be easy to pick Mary apart, but the girl really does know how to suck dick."

"I wonder how Faelan will feel watching it."

"I actually think that's the reason Kylie is okay with the scene. Faelan said when he viewed it, he felt like he was seeing two people he vaguely knew performing a scene together. He felt so detached that he could actually appreciate the scene without feeling any emotions about it."

"Huh...I don't think I'll ever get to that point. If I saw Liam again, I would be a total basket case." She shivered. "But Faelan's way more mature than I'll ever be."

Brie bumped hips with Lea. "Don't knock yourself, girlfriend. You were put through hell and lied to. Faelan, on the other hand, knew exactly what he was walking into when he collared Mary."

"True..."

Brie looked at the last remaining seats and frowned, trying to remember whom it was that she was forgetting.

"Oh, yeah! Master Coen."

"What? Master Coen is coming all the way up from Australia?"

Brie nodded enthusiastically. "He sure is. I told him I was going to do the screening and offered to send him a copy, but he insisted on coming up in person."

"Oh, my goodness! It's going to be amazing to see him again. All those giant muscles attached to one gorgeous body…"

Brie laughed. "His body is definitely one you don't forget."

"I wonder if he's picked up an Australian accent. Can you imagine anything hotter?"

Brie grinned. "I'd be shocked if he picked up an accent that quickly, but I agree it would be smoking hot."

Lea started jumping up and down excitedly. "I can't believe we're going to have everyone gathered all under one roof. You've got all the trainers and the three musketeers from the original class. The only one missing is Mr. Gallant."

"Actually, that's the last two seats. I invited Ena and Mr. Gallant even though they are not in the film because he was so supportive of the first film."

"The entire Submissive Training Center gang together again in one place!" Lea bumped her hip against Brie so enthusiastically that Brie stumbled before she regained her balance.

"With a few extra friends we gained along the way," Brie added. She decided to bring up the subject of Ms. Clark. "Are you sure you're okay knowing Ms. Clark is coming tonight?"

Lea snorted. "Umm...actually, Samantha and I recently started talking again."

"You have?" Brie asked, unable to hide her shock.

"Yeah. She knew I'd be here, and called to ask if I would mind if she came."

"Really? Wow, that's thoughtful of her."

"She's a good person, Brie," Lea stated.

Brie suddenly felt unsettled, now worried for Lea.

Lea smiled at her knowingly. "I can tell exactly what you're thinking, Stinky Cheese. Yes, Samantha broke up with me, but I don't hate her for it. It would be ridiculous to spend the rest of our lives avoiding each other."

"As long as you're good with it, girlfriend. Really, that's all that matters to me."

"I'm doing just fine," Lea assured her. "But man, we sure have complicated lives. I can't believe everything that's happened since we graduated from the Center. I swear you could make a blockbuster movie out of it."

Brie laughed. "We'll call it, *The Ongoing Adventures of the Submissive Training Center Gang.*"

"Not nearly enough pizzazz, girlfriend! Why don't we call it something like *Three Musketeers of Submission — The Ongoing Story of Lea the Lovely, Brie the Bodacious and Mary the Magnificent.* That should get people's attention."

"You don't think that title is a tad long?"

"Oh, okay. How about *The TMoS — Lea the Lovely, Brie the Bodacious and Mary the Mag.*"

"Mag?"

"Yeah, you know. Short for magnificent."

Brie laughed. "You are all kinds of weird, Lea. But that's what I love about you."

"And this girl loves you, Stinky Cheese." Lea gave Brie a tight squeeze. "You know what?"

"What?"

"Thinking about all of us being together again has made me realize something."

"Oh, yeah?"

"Liam may have ripped my fucking heart out, but he didn't change who I am. Before I met him, I was doing just fine. I had my pick of whomever Dom or Domme I wanted to scene with, and any kind of new kink I wanted to try."

"You are very popular at the clubs," Brie agreed.

"I'm not going to let what happened to me change the path I am on."

"You sounded very Tono-esque just then."

Lea smiled. "Yeah, Tono would definitely encourage me to reclaim what's mine, and breathe the shit all over it."

Brie giggled. "I can just imagine him saying that." Speaking with Tono's peaceful manner, she said solemnly, "Just breathe the shit all over it."

The two of them kept giggling while they continued setting up and then let out a hearty cheer when Sir and Rytsar arrived with the equipment.

It seemed appropriate that Tono and Autumn should be the first to arrive. Brie invited them inside, gushing excitedly, "I'm so happy you're here."

Seeing Tono's gentle smile and chocolate brown eyes instantly brought a sense of peace to her soul. "It is an honor to be here tonight. We've been anxious to see this latest work of yours."

Brie smiled at them both. "I think you guys are going to love the first scene in the film."

"Oh, why is that?" Autumn asked.

"Because it stars Tono and Lea, of course!"

They were still laughing when Lea came up behind Autumn and covered her eyes. "Guess who."

Autumn grinned. "I don't know, but I've got a joke for whoever it is."

"Give it to me."

"What did the cracker say to the stinky cheese?"

"Do tell."

"We Brie long together."

Lea howled with laughter, elbowing Brie several times. "Oh, my goodness, is Autumn funny or what? 'We Brie long together...' You kill me, girl!"

Autumn giggled, confessing to Brie, "I've been saving that one for a while.

When Lea finally stopped laughing, she shot a joke at Autumn. "Last night, there was a seminar on how to withhold orgasms. Guess what?"

"What?" Autumn asked, grinning.

"Nobody came!" Lea went off on another laughing jag.

Brie shook her head, laughing at the two of them.

Tono glanced at the orchid in Brie's hair. "You still wear it."

"Of course, I do," she said, touching the petals. "It

reminds me to breathe. I don't do any filming without it."

He smiled graciously. "You are pleased with this film, Brie?"

She leaned in and whispered, "I think it's my best work yet."

He nodded proudly. "I would expect no less from you."

Brie had always felt a strong connection with Tono. The time and distance hadn't changed that, although the dynamic of their relationship had changed. Looking at Autumn, who was laughing hysterically with Lea, Brie noticed that she was completely oblivious to the long scar that covered the right side of her face.

"You have made great strides with Autumn since you collared her. She's like a whole new person."

"No," he said gazing at the woman with love. "The change has all been from her, I was simply the conduit."

"So, do you think she's ready to perform in front of a live audience yet?"?"

"Yes. In fact, our first performance will be in LA in January. I would like to send you and Sir Davis tickets to attend."

"Oh, Tono, we wouldn't miss that for the world!"

He glanced around the great room, taking in the impressive view of the ocean. "This is an auspicious occasion for you. I—"

Shadow suddenly appeared and walked straight to Tono, ignoring everyone else in the room. Tono knelt down to pet the cat. "It has been a long time, Shadow."

"He's missed you." Brie was touched by the cat's affection for the Asian Dom.

"I have missed him, as well." Tono smiled up at her—a smile that still made Brie's heart burst with joy.

"Nosaka, it's good to see you again." Sir said, walking up to greet him, holding out his hand. "This screening would not be complete without you."

Tono stood, much to Shadow's disappointment, to shake his hand. "As you know, Autumn and I are big fans of your wife's work." He smiled at Brie. "Nothing could keep us away."

"Would you like a tour of the house?" Sir asked him.

"Sure." Tono picked up the huge black cat, who was purring loudly. "I would love to see it."

Brie was about to join them when the doorbell rang.

She shrugged, excusing herself. "I guess the party has officially begun…"

A half hour later, Brie stood in front of her friends and trainers, feeling like a bundle of nerves. When she couldn't stop her hands from trembling, she put them behind her back so no one would notice and smiled at everyone.

"First, I'd like to thank everyone for coming tonight. It means so much to have you here for this very first showing of my new documentary."

Her friends smiled at her from their seats, and she felt the nerves beginning to ease.

Looking over at Master Coen, Brie bowed her head.

"It's an honor to have Master Coen travel such a long distance to join us."

Everyone clapped, welcoming him back.

"Wouldn't miss it for the world, Mrs. Davis," he told her. "I hope you don't mind, but I plan to live-stream the film so that raven can see her performance since she was unable to make the trip with me."

"Of course, Master Coen. I hope raven enjoys it."

Looking at Boa next, Brie gushed, "I'm deeply grateful to Boa for preparing an incredible array of food for the party. When he offered to bring a few hors d'oeuvres, I never expected to be treated to such a wide variety of delicious tapas. It reminds me of our Submissive Training Center days during our breaks from the class."

Boa grinned. "That's exactly what I was going for."

"Well, you've taken this evening to another level. Thank you."

Mistress Lou patted Boa's thigh, clearly proud of her sub.

"As you guys know, I've been working tirelessly to edit this film for release. While this is by no means the final product, this is my vision of what it will look like. However, I'm certainly open to suggestions once you've watched the documentary in its entirety. Please understand that it's important to me that you feel the part you are featured in does you and the scene justice."

Brie played with the white orchid in her hair, glancing at Tono.

"My intention with this second film is to show the wide variety of experiences that can be explored under the BDSM umbrella, and I wanted to present it in a way that would entertain and educate people at the same time. By watching the various scenes play out, I hope people will not only identify with the sensual aspect of BDSM but also the connection that comes from it. I truly want the quality of each scene to speak for itself."

Brie took a deep breath and let it out slowly. "So…without further ado, I present my latest work with much thanks to all of you."

She bowed low before sitting down between Sir and Rytsar. Brie had chosen her seat placement purposely so she could observe everyone's reactions while watching the film.

When Sir pressed the button on the remote and the lights dimmed, Brie held her breath as her film began.

The deep base of the dubstep she had chosen was meant to instantly grab the audience and suck them in. Looking at her friends' reactions, she could see it was doing just that.

Brie found it interesting how her friends had paired up. She wasn't surprised to see Tono, Lea, and Autumn sitting together because they were good friends.

She also wasn't surprised that Captain, Candy, and Baron sat side by side. Although Captain and Candy had no part in the film, Brie had invited them for two reasons. She knew Baron would value their presence here tonight, but she had also done it for Mary and it warmed her heart to see Mary seated in between Captain and Candy.

Faelan and Kylie had chosen to sit a row back, but they still seemed comfortable to be in close proximity to

Mary. Brie found that encouraging. The fact that Marquis and Celestia were sitting next to Faelan seemed only natural. The mutual admiration the two Doms had for each other was well known in the community.

Mistress Lou and Boa had paired up with Master Anderson and Shay. Although Shay was not part of the BDSM community, as far as Brie knew, she definitely seemed comfortable sitting next to the Asian Domme and her male sub.

In the farthest row, Ms. Clark had chosen to sit with the Gallants. Everyone in attendance knew that Rytsar had forgiven Ms. Clark, but Brie suspected it must still have been hard for Ms. Clark to come. Thankfully, Mr. Gallant and Ena were the perfect ambassadors, and Ms. Clark actually seemed relaxed as she sat there and watched.

Brie sighed in contentment, thrilled to have their house full of the people who had helped shape her into the woman she was. Each person had played a significant role in her life and had come here now to support her dreams. It gave her happy goosebumps.

With the film starting, Brie was finally able to shake off the nerves. She was proud of this film. This was exactly where she wanted to be, and what she wanted to be doing.

There was no reason to feel anything but excitement.

Sitting back in her chair, Brie watched as the movie opened up with Tono's scene with Lea, leading with a voiceover as Tono explained the philosophy behind Kinbaku and the vision he had for his unique adaptation of the art.

A tear came to her eye as the haunting flute music filled the room. She watched the scene unfold, ending with Lea flying in the jute. It was that much more moving to Brie to know that Autumn had been present at that filming. Looking at the three of them sitting together, Brie was suddenly struck by the thought that they would make a really cute threesome.

The film continued moving from scene to scene, building in intensity as they watched Master Coen's spanking session with raven and the sensual oral scene between Faelan and Mary.

Brie snuck glances at them, trying not to be obvious. She noticed Faelan and Kylie watching it with casual interest, while Mary kept shifting in her seat. It was definitely having an effect on her.

After that stimulating scene ended, Baron's sultry voice rang out in a voiceover as he explained the purpose and correct use of punishment in the D/s dynamic. Brie enjoyed watching the sensual reenactment of her first sex-swing lesson with Baron and smiled at him when it was over.

With the audience warmed up, it was time for Ms. Clark's session with her male and female sub. Watching the seductive manner in which she played out the scene with both subs was truly inspiring, reminding Brie of why Samantha had earned the devotion of so many through the years.

When Brie glanced at her, she was surprised to see Ms. Clark looking straight at her. The Domme nodded her head. Brie turned back to the film in shock. Ms. Clark liked her scene!

Sir put his hand on her knee and squeezed it, while Rytsar whispered in a low voice, "Powerful."

Brie felt like her heart would burst with happiness.

Master Anderson's bullwhip scene with Boa came next. Even though she had spent countless hours editing the piece, it was so provocative that it still had the power to make Brie wet.

She heard several soft gasps while the scene played out, letting her know that the others were being similarly affected. Something about watching Master Anderson's undeniable skill with the bullwhip automatically evoked a response.

Rytsar grinned when he saw that his scene was next. "I remember it as if it were yesterday," he murmured to her. No voiceover was needed with this part because Rytsar had done an excellent job of explaining the nature of his dominance over the sub as he scened. Brie could feel the girl's genuine terror as she looked at the electric instrument he held, but it was clear that her need outweighed her fear, when the audience watched her willingly press her nipple against the instrument as she cried out in pain.

Her submission to Rytsar's sadistic dominance was unique and fascinating to watch.

Brie smiled when Marquis Gray's scene began. This was the one Holloway had cut from the film when they first met to talk about it. However, Brie felt it was one of the most powerful scenes in the entire film. The grace of Marquis' movements as he wielded the eighty-tailed flogger was extraordinary to watch. But, what made the scene even more powerful was the connection Brie had with Marquis. That connection was tangible on the screen, and his voiceover describing the importance of trust was truly moving.

Brie had chosen to end the documentary with her interview with Mr. Gannon, which he had given when she'd visited his commune called the Sanctuary. While he shared his reasons for creating the commune, Brie peppered the scene with cutaway shots showcasing the natural beauty of the large estate and the diversity of people who lived there.

"I used all of my investments to build The Sanctuary in 2001. Our community lives off the grid, and each person is required to help maintain the estate to meet the needs of all of its members.

"The vetting process is quite lengthy to ensure everyone shares my vision and has skills that can be utilized by the community as a whole.

"We share everything together, including our kinks," Gannon said, smiling at the camera. "You would be surprised by how satisfying sex can be when societal limitations are stripped away."

His expression became more thoughtful when he shared, "It all comes down to a matter of trust. Here at the Sanctuary, I insist that the people eat dinner together. It's during mealtimes that connections are made and cemented. We are not just a bunch of kinksters, but a true community in every sense of the word."

Hearing his voice, Shadow suddenly appeared and ran up to the screen. He sat, watching his late Master, slowly wagging his tail back and forth. Brie had to hold back the tears. She knew how much Shadow must still miss him.

The film ended with Gannon's wish for the future. "I hope my vision will inspire other communes like it. America has been bound by laws created by prudish misfits. It is time to open our minds and bodies to something greater."

The credits ended with an "in memoriam" for Gannon and the lights came up.

The room was silent. Brie felt a moment of panic as the seconds ticked by, then watched in surprise as everyone stood up and began to clap.

"You have wowed us all, babygirl," Sir said with pride, kissing her on the lips.

Rytsar picked her up, laughing. "A masterpiece, *radost moya!*"

Brie was overwhelmed by her friends' many accolades but waited with bated breath to hear what Marquis Gray thought.

He did not approach her until the others had spoken with her, and then asked if he could speak to her in private. Brie felt her stomach twist into a knot but immediately agreed, escorting him to Sir's office.

After she shut the door, Brie turned to face him and asked, "What is your honest opinion about the film, Marquis?"

"My honest opinion? I do not think you should work with Holloway."

Brie was taken aback. She wondered how much Marquis knew of Holloway and Mary's history.

Marquis' gaze was intense when he added, "But if you must, do not give an inch. Not. One. Inch."

Brie couldn't believe it. "Thank you, Marquis. That means so much to me!"

"You have a true vision, Mrs. Davis. Do not compromise it."

Brie nodded, too stunned to speak.

Marquis reached for the door. "Before Boa's hard work goes to waste, let's sample the bounty he has created in honor of your work."

Brie walked out of the office feeling as if she were floating on air. Lea and Mary came running up to find out what he'd said.

"He liked it," Brie said in disbelief. "He told me not to change a thing."

Mary slugged her arm. "I told you. We got this in the bag, Stinks."

"But he did warn me *not* to work with Holloway."

"Oh, yeah, I'm not surprised. Those two had a huge falling out recently, but we can't let that stop us. This is bigger than them. It's bigger than all of us," Mary told her.

Brie hugged her, deeply touched that Mary felt that way.

"As soon as this one is released, you can get started on our motion picture," Lea said with a giggle.

"What motion picture?" Mary asked, frowning.

Brie laughed. "Oh, Lea was thinking I should do a movie about the three of us and all the crazy shit that's happened in our lives."

"You know what they say, truth is stranger than fiction," Lea piped up.

Mary snorted. "Fuck, ain't that the truth."

"I was telling Brie that we should call it *Three Musketeers of Submission – The Ongoing Story of Lea the Lovely, Brie the Bodacious, and Mary the Magnificent.*"

Mary huffed. "That would never fly. Way too long, but I've got a title for ya."

"Okay, shoot," Lea encouraged her.

Mary arched her eyebrow. "Why don't we call it *Stinkz?* It's like *Cats*, but it's about a submissive and nobody dies at the end."

Brie and Lea broke out in peals of laughter.

Sir came walking over, smiling, "What's so funny?"

"Nothing, Sir Davis," Mary assured him. "As you know, Lea and Brie have no sense of humor and will laugh at anything."

Sir smirked at Mary. Turning to Brie, he held out his arm. "Your presence has been requested."

He walked her to the kitchen where Rytsar was already lining up shots to toast the film.

Rytsar raised his glass to Brie. "May your documentaries live on forever and give our future generations, like *moye solntse*, hope that no matter what path she chooses sexually, she will be accepted and loved for who she is."

Everyone raised their glasses enthusiastically and drank to the toast.

Brie smiled as she looked at all the people gathered around her.

Although she knew she'd have a tough fight getting this film out in theaters, she had a deep sense of pride knowing her work had given them a voice—and that voice was powerful and beautiful.

I hope you enjoyed *Tied to Hope: Brie's Submission!*
COMING UP NEXT—*Hope's First Christmas: Brie's Submission Novella*

The next book in the Brie Series

Yes, you heard me right.

This November!

Read the next book of Brie!

(Release Date – Nov 5, 2019)

~~~~~~~

** You can begin the journey of Sir, Rytsar and Master Anderson when they first met!**

Start reading Sir's Rise the 1st book in the Rise of the Dominants Trilogy

COMING NEXT

Hope's First Christmas:
Brie's Submission Novella
Available for Preorder

Reviews mean the world to me!

I truly appreciate you taking the time to review
Tied to Hope.

If you could leave a review on both Goodreads and the
site where you purchased this book from, I would be so
grateful. Sincerely, ~Red

You can begin the journey of Sir, Rytsar and Master
Anderson when they first met with *Sir's Rise* the 1st book
in the *Rise of the Dominants Series*!

Start reading NOW!

ABOUT THE AUTHOR

Over Two Million readers have enjoyed Red's stories

Red Phoenix – USA Today Bestselling Author
Winner of 8 Readers' Choice Awards

Hey Everyone!

I'm Red Phoenix, an author who also happens to be a submissive in real life. I wrote the Brie's Submission series because I wanted people everywhere to know just how much fun BDSM can be.

There is a huge cast of characters who are part of Brie's journey. The further you read into the story the more you learn about each one. I hope you grow to love Brie and the gang as much as I do.

They've become like family.

When I'm not writing, you can find me online with readers.

I heart my fans! ~Red

To find out more visit my Website
redphoenixauthor.com
Follow Me on BookBub
bookbub.com/authors/red-phoenix
Newsletter: Sign up
redphoenixauthor.com/newsletter-signup
Facebook: AuthorRedPhoenix
Twitter: @redphoenix69
Instagram: RedPhoenixAuthor
I invite you to join my reader Group!
facebook.com/groups/539875076052037

SIGN UP FOR MY NEWSLETTER
HERE FOR THE LATEST RED
PHOENIX UPDATES

SALES, GIVEAWAYS, NEW
RELEASES, EXCLUSIVE SNEAK
PEEKS, AND MORE!
SIGN UP HERE
REDPHOENIXAUTHOR.COM/NEWSLETTER-
SIGNUP

Red Phoenix is the author of:

Brie's Submission Series:
Teach Me #1
Love Me #2
Catch Me #3
Try Me #4
Protect Me #5
Hold Me #6
Surprise Me #7
Trust Me #8
Claim Me #9
Enchant Me #10
A Cowboy's Heart #11
Breathe with Me #12
Her Russian Knight #13
Under His Protection #14
Her Russian Returns #15
In Sir's Arms #16
Bound by Love #17
Tied to Hope #18
Hope's First Christmas #19

*You can also purchase the AUDIO BOOK **Versions**

Also part of the Submissive Training Center world:

Captain's Duet
Safe Haven #1
Destined to Dominate #2

Rise of the Dominates Trilogy
Sir's Rise #1
Master's Fate #2
The Russian Reborn #3

Other Books by Red Phoenix

Blissfully Undone
* Available in eBook and paperback

(Snowy Fun—Two people find themselves snowbound in a cabin where hidden love can flourish, taking one couple on a sensual journey into ménage à trois)

His Scottish Pet: Dom of the Ages
* Available in eBook and paperback

Audio Book: *His Scottish Pet: Dom of the Ages*

(Scottish Dom—A sexy Dom escapes to Scotland in the late 1400s. He encounters a waif who has the potential to free him from his tragic curse)

The Erotic Love Story of Amy and Troy
* Available in eBook and paperback

(Sexual Adventures—True love reigns, but fate continually throws Troy and Amy into the arms of others)

eBooks

Varick: The Reckoning

(Savory Vampire—A dark, sexy vampire story. The hero navigates the dangerous world he has been thrust into with lusty passion and a pure heart)

Keeper of the Wolf Clan (Keeper of Wolves, #1)

(Sexual Secrets—A virginal werewolf must act as the clan's mysterious Keeper)

The Keeper Finds Her Mate (Keeper of Wolves, #2)

(Second Chances—A young she-wolf must choose between old ties or new beginnings)

The Keeper Unites the Alphas (Keeper of Wolves, #3)

(Serious Consequences—The young she-wolf is captured by the rival clan)

Boxed Set: Keeper of Wolves Series (Books 1-3)

(Surprising Secrets—A secret so shocking it will rock Layla's world. The young she-wolf is put in a position of being able to save her werewolf clan or becoming the reason for its destruction)

Socrates Inspires Cherry to Blossom

(Satisfying Surrender—A mature and curvaceous woman becomes fascinated by an online Dom who has much to teach her)

By the Light of the Scottish Moon

(Saving Love—Two lost souls, the Moon, a werewolf, and a death wish…)

In 9 Days

(Sweet Romance—A young girl falls in love with the new student, nicknamed "the Freak")

---

9 Days and Counting

(Sacrificial Love—The sequel to *In 9 Days* delves into the emotional reunion of two longtime lovers)

And Then He Saved Me

(Saving Tenderness—When a young girl tries to kill herself, a man of great character intervenes with a love that heals)

Play With Me at Noon

(Seeking Fulfillment—A desperate wife lives out her fantasies by taking five different men in five days)

Connect with Red on Substance B

Substance B is a platform for independent authors to directly connect with their readers. Please visit Red's Substance B page where you can:

- Sign up for Red's newsletter
- Send a message to Red
- See all platforms where Red's books are sold

Visit Substance B today to learn more about your favorite independent authors.